HORSES O

*H*ALF *M*OON
RANCH

MOONDANCE

Horses of Half-Moon Ranch 1: Wild Horses
Horses of Half-Moon Ranch 2: Rodeo Rocky
Horses of Half-Moon Ranch 3: Crazy Horse
Horses of Half-Moon Ranch 4: Johnny Mohawk
Horses of Half-Moon Ranch 5: Midnight Lady
Horses of Half-Moon Ranch 6: Third-Time Lucky
Horses of Half-Moon Ranch 7: Navaho Joe
Horses of Half-Moon Ranch 8: Hollywood Princess
Horses of Half-Moon Ranch 9: Danny Boy
Horses of Half-Moon Ranch 10: Little Vixen
Horses of Half-Moon Ranch 11: Gunsmoke
Horses of Half-Moon Ranch 12: Golden Dawn
Horses of Half-Moon Ranch 13: Silver Spur
Horses of Half-Moon Ranch Summer Special: Jethro Junior
Horses of Half-Moon Ranch Christmas Special: Starlight

Home Farm Twins 1–20
Home Farm Twins Christmas Special: Scruffy The Scamp
Home Farm Twins Summer Special: Stanley The Troublemaker
Home Farm Twins Christmas Special: Smoky The Mystery
Home Farm Twins Summer Special: Stalky The Mascot
Home Farm Twins Christmas Special: Samantha The Snob
Home Farm Twins Christmas Special: Smarty The Outcast
Home Farm Friends: Short Story Collection

Animal Alert 1–10
Animal Alert Summer Special: Heatwave
Animal Alert Christmas Special: Lost and Found

One for Sorrow
Two for Joy
Three for a Girl
Four for a Boy
Five for Silver
Six for Gold
Seven for a Secret
Eight for a Wish
Nine for a Kiss

MOONDANCE

JENNY OLDFIELD

Illustrated by
Paul Hunt

Hodder
Children's
Books

a division of Hodder Headline Limited

With thanks to Bob, Karen and Katie Foster, and to the staff and
guests at Lost Valley Ranch, Deckers, Colorado

First published in Great Britain in 2001
by Hodder Children's Books

A Catalogue record for this book is available from the British Library

ISBN 0 340 79170 5

Typeset by Avon Dataset Ltd, Bidford-on-Avon, Warks

Printed and bound in Great Britain by
The Guernsey Press Co. Ltd, Channel Isles

Hodder Children's Books
a division of Hodder Headline Limited
338 Euston Road
London NW1 3BH

1

'That'll be three coffees and two OJs, plus five breakfasts with hash-browns and eggs over-easy!' Lisa Goodman wrote down the order from the five guys sitting at a table by the door at the End of Trail Diner.

Kirstie Scott took it easy. She sat at the counter, sipping an ice-cold Coke and gazing out at the busy Main Street. She saw pick-ups drive by loaded with fence posts, razor wire, horse tack and farming equipment. Beaten-up saloons dropped off kids for their Saturday shopping sprees. Trailers trundled slowly towards the out-of-town sale barn. Just the usual San Luis weekend bustle – ranchers filling up with gas at the Esso station, women crowding into the one and only supermarket, horse traders stopping off at the diner for one of Bonnie Goodman's famous Big Breakfasts.

'Make my bacon extra crispy!' one of the ranch hands called to Lisa, tipping back on to two legs of his chair. His long legs sprawled wide and his metal spurs chinked on the wooden floor.

'Gotcha!' Lisa nodded. 'Hey, Kirstie, how about you lend a hand here?'

'Hey, I'm a customer, remember!' Kirstie protested.

Lisa thrust a steaming coffee pot into her hand. 'Yeah, and I'm run off my feet. Mom just drove down to the sale barn with a take-out order for hamburgers. I need you to pour those guys their coffee!'

'Jeez!' Kirstie grumbled without really meaning it. Actually, she was glad to be busy. It took her mind off the fact that three of the yearlings from Half-Moon Ranch were at this very moment going through the sale barn. The wrench of having to sell them was giving her a hard time. So she went to pour the coffee.

'You got extra cream?' one guy asked.

'Hey, and bring me french toast with plenty of maple syrup.'

'More orange juice for me.'

The guys had Kirstie on a yo-yo string, while Lisa fried their bacon real crisp.

'The boss say anythin' to you about takin' a day off?' the long-legged one asked the other hands. All were lean, tanned and in need of a shave, dressed in jeans, plaid shirts and dusty cowboy boots. Their stetson hats hung from the backs of their chairs.

'Nope,' came the reply.

'The boss ain't heard of days off,' one joked. 'The way he sees it, we work twenty-four hours a day, eight days a week!'

'Bacon, hash-browns and eggs over-easy!' Lisa came with their cooked orders.

'You got tomato sauce?'

'Can you rustle up some more coffee?'

'Gee, these hash-browns taste good!'

At last, the five demanding customers tucked into their breakfasts.

'Phew!' Lisa wiped her hot brow as she and Kirstie retreated behind the counter.

'Where did those guys drive in from?' Kirstie wanted to know.

Lisa shrugged, then stole another look. 'I never seen them before. That young one in the blue shirt is kinda cute, though!'

Kirstie raised her eyebrows at her bubbly, red-haired friend. Lisa was always joking around.

'Yeah, well you wouldn't notice!' Lisa teased. 'If it doesn't walk around on four legs and have a long mane and tail, Kirstie Scott ain't interested!'

Before Kirstie could come up with a good reply, the door of the diner opened and two more men walked in. One carried an expensive-looking camera and a bag of equipment. The other followed him in, making the kind of grand entrance that couldn't be ignored. He was tall and broad shouldered, dressed in a cream shirt and matching stetson. His jeans were starched, his tan leather boots classy and new.

'Hey, boss!' The five men eating breakfast stopped mid-chew. They scraped back their chairs to make room for the well-dressed newcomer. The kid in the blue shirt stood up and offered his seat. The 'boss' sat down without saying thanks, while the guy with the camera came over to the counter. 'Just a couple of strong black coffees,' he told Lisa.

'Comin' right up!' Her eyes shone with

excitement as she turned to the coffee machine. 'Wow!' she hissed.

'Steve, get your butt over here!' the big man ordered in a loud voice. 'We got a deal to discuss!' The photographer sighed and did as he was told.

'Who is that guy?' Kirstie whispered to Lisa. She'd taken an instant dislike to him, despite his movie-star looks.

Lisa turned to her in disbelief. 'You don't recognise him?' Kirstie shook her head. She looked again. The 'boss' was maybe thirty years old, with short black hair and a square, clean-shaven face. His eyebrows were dark and straight, the eyes beneath a pale shade of brown.

'Hey, and you're the horse expert!' Lisa teased as the coffee machine hissed and steamed. ' "That guy", as you call him, is *only* Ty Turner. They just made a movie about him and a horse called Firefly. I have the video right here in my room!'

The name Ty Turner did mean something to Kirstie. She was still thinking about the big-mouth in the diner as she made her way down Main Street towards the sale barn to join her mom and Hadley Crane. Turner had hit the headlines recently as the latest trainer to claim that he'd discovered a new method of working with problem horses.

True, these guys with magical new training techniques were springing up everywhere, because there was big money in running special clinics that attracted huge audiences. But the unusual thing about Turner's method was that it had set up a name for never turning away a horse, however bad the problem. 'There ain't no such thing as a mean horse. Only a mean owner' was his slogan. And the message was reaching hundreds of thousands of horse lovers by means of the Firefly movie that Lisa had mentioned.

Older cowboys and ranch hands, like Hadley for instance, didn't set a lot of store by men like Turner. 'Not that I belong to the old "buck 'em out, make 'em mind" way of thinking,' Hadley had said when Turner's name had come up in conversation recently. 'I don't believe in bein' cruel to an animal any more than the next guy. I only say that Turner's jumpin' on a bandwagon and claimin' things that ain't true.'

Anyway, Kirstie's older brother Matt had said they had another reason to be wary of Ty Turner at Half-Moon Ranch, even though they'd never met him.

'He just bought Waddie Newton's spread at Aspen

Park,' Matt had reported. 'From what I hear, Turner plans to set up a dude ranch out there. And given all the free publicity he got from the Firefly thing, I reckon folks are gonna be turnin' away from us and choosin' to spend their vacations at Aspen Park instead!'

'I just ran into Ty Turner in Bonnie's diner,' Kirstie told her mom and Hadley. She'd met up with them beside the sale ring, having woven her way through row after row of empty trailers and pushed her way through a crush of people.

'Say that again!' Sandy Scott yelled above the machine-gun rattle of the auctioneer's voice and the nervous whinnies of half a dozen horses still waiting to be led into the ring.

'I said, I saw Ty Turner!' she repeated. 'He came into the End of Trail Diner.'

'Save it till later, OK?' Sandy stood on tiptoe to see the latest colt to come under the auctioneer's hammer. It was a brown-and-white paint with the quarter-horse's typical sturdy conformation: strong in the hindquarters, with short legs and big head.

'Did our yearlings come through yet?' Kirstie asked Hadley, hoping that the answer would be yes.

The old man shook his head. 'They're next in line.'

Bad timing! Kirstie thought. Over the past year Sparky, Cutter and Butterscotch had become part of the scene at Half-Moon Ranch and she hated to see them go. On the other hand, being here would allow her to watch them find good new homes. She hoped.

'Sold to Wes Logan for two hundred and fifty dollars!' Bud Morris, the auctioneer, quickly disposed of the paint colt. 'Next, I want y'all to take a real good look at three yearlings from the Half-Moon ramuda, to be sold as one lot . . .' Kirstie braced herself as a couple of sale barn assistants led in their babies. The three young horses looked startled and ill at ease, ears laid back, heads raised and pulling at their lead-ropes.

'Now I don't need to remind you folks that any horse from Sandy Scott's string has a nice nature and a good bloodline.' Morris talked them up with his rapid-fire delivery. 'These will make great kiddy horses. They should reach no more than thirteen or fourteen hands and there ain't a bad bone in their bodies. Now, what am I bid for these three little honeys?'

Looking anxiously around the ring, Kirstie noted

that a few hands went up with offers to take all three colts together. One of the bidders was Donna Rose from a neighbouring ranch. Another was a woman with a couple of teenage kids whom Kirstie didn't recognise. A third was a hard-headed dealer from out of state.

As Bud led the bidding towards a fast conclusion, Kirstie found herself willing Donna Rose to come out the winner. After all, her spread at the Circle R was close enough to visit. And if Kirstie were ever to wonder how the yearlings were settling in, she knew that there would always be a warm welcome from the lady ranch boss.

'Eleven hundred, eleven-fifty, twelve. Any more?' Bud paused with his hammer raised. He looked quickly around the ring. Who had offered the twelve hundred dollars? Kirstie couldn't be sure. She just had to hope it wasn't the dealer from New Mexico.

Bud brought down his hammer with a sharp tap. 'Sold to Donna Rose for twelve hundred bucks!' Kirstie heaved a sigh of relief. Donna grinned from the opposite side of the ring, well satisfied with the deal.

'So we can relax and head for home.' Sandy voiced their thoughts. Like Kirstie, she hated to part with any of their stock. But Half-Moon Ranch was a business, Matt always reminded her. And part of it was to sell on the horses they didn't need.

Sandy, Kirstie and Hadley were slowly making their way through the dense crowd when Bud Morris asked for the next horse to be led in.

As it happened, their route towards their empty trailer took them close to the narrow chute containing the horses still to be sold. Kirstie caught a glimpse of a blue-grey roan tugging away from the handler's grasp, half-rearing above the wooden boards and refusing to go into the ring.

'Next in line is a real classy blue roan mare!' Bud Morris announced.

'Quit it!' the handler told the mare in a rough voice. He seemed to land a blow which swiftly brought the horse back to a standing position.

Kirstie frowned. She saw Hadley half turn as if to say something to the handler, then think better of it.

'You two comin'?' Sandy asked.

'Let's wait and see how this one goes,' Kirstie suggested. Blue roans were her latest favourite colour – after palominos, of course.

'What for?' Sandy asked.

'No reason,' she hedged.

'We've done all our business for today,' Sandy

warned, not trusting the innocent look Kirstie gave her.

'I know. Hadley and I just want to watch,' she insisted. 'Don't we, Hadley?'

'Uh-huh,' he grunted, making his way back to the edge of the ring with Kirstie close on his heels.

'Four years old, from the Aspen Park ramuda, this lady is a real beauty!' Bud enthused.

This time he didn't have to work to get the crowd's attention. All eyes were already on the mare as she emerged with her handler from the chute. She was fifteen hands and coloured a dappled, smoky grey, with a pale mane and tail. Rangier than most quarter-horses, she was built like a plains horse, for speed rather than stamina. And her head had a touch of mustang about her in the flared nostrils and high carriage.

'This mare has a lot of breeding behind her,' the auctioneer went on, sensing from the interest already roused that he could achieve a high price. 'She has more than a hundred days on her, so all the hard work is done. Right now she'd make a fine horse for the more experienced type of rider – someone who can recognise a good piece of horse-flesh.'

Kirstie climbed on the bottom rung of the fence

to appreciate the blue roan's high-stepping walk. 'That's some horse!' she breathed.

'Kirstie!' Sandy warned. 'Don't even think about it!' Hadley stood quietly to one side as Sandy made it clear that no way were they in the market to buy another horse.

Meanwhile, Bud Morris looked down at a note on his desk. 'This here piece of paper tells me that the mare's name is Moondance, out of Moonwalker. The bloodline goes way back to some fine pro-rodeo broncs. In other words, ladies and gentlemen, this is one rare opportunity to buy a quality mount!'

As he talked, Kirstie's gaze was fixed on the blue roan. There was a spring in every step, pride in the arch of her neck, but a lot of nervous tension in the clench of her jaw and tight nostrils. No wonder, she thought; the horse just took a heavy kick or punch back there in the chute.

'What say we start the bidding at two thousand five hundred?' Bud suggested, confident that he could push up the price way past three thousand.

He took bids for two-five, two-seven-fifty, two-eight as the handler completed one whole circuit of the small arena.

Then the orderly world of the sale barn was ripped apart. Moondance had done one complete circle around the ring when she went crazy. With a sudden shrill whinny, she went up on her hind legs, her front hooves pawing the air and flailing down towards the handler. He fought back for a second, then let go of the rope and vaulted out of the ring to safety. Landing on all fours, the mare began to kick out and buck, the loose lead-rope flailing. She snaked her back to kick sideways, thudding against the fence and making the onlookers back off in fear. Then she loped wildly round the ring, kicking up dust and dirt, screeching out a wild protest at being trapped inside this hostile circle of faces and hats.

'Hey Bud, forget that bid of two thousand eight hundred,' a bidder yelled above the thunder of hooves. 'There's one helluva mean streak in that critter!'

'Likewise!' the other interested parties called. 'No way do we wanna lay out good money on a horse that can't be rode!'

'I thought Bud said she had over a hundred days of work behind her?' someone else put in, shaking his head. 'Jeez, I wouldn't like to be the cowboy who had to get up on her back and ride out after a bunch of steers!'

The auctioneer had now called for two wranglers

on horseback to come into the ring. They rode with ropes, swinging their lassos at the blue roan until one got a fix on her head and neck, while the other trapped a back leg in his noose.

The ropes brought the mare crashing down. She lay in the dirt breathing heavily for a few seconds, then struggled back to her feet. She lashed out violently with her back legs, only to find herself tethered and half strangled.

'I wish they'd quit that!' Kirstie muttered, almost able to feel the mare's pain in her own body. 'Why don't they just get her out of here and give her time to calm down?'

Bud Morris cleared his throat. When he started to speak again, there was a different tone. 'OK, so the mare has a few problems,' he conceded. 'But it ain't nothing that can't be smoothed out with a little work. What say we take the bidding down a couple of notches? Who'll give me fifteen hundred dollars?'

No response from the crowd. They'd all been too close to Moondance's flying hooves to risk putting in a bid. 'It don't matter how pretty a horse is,' a woman near to Kirstie pointed out. 'If the temperament is suspect, you'd be a fool to take her on!'

Kirstie frowned at how suddenly the thing had turned around. A few minutes earlier, before the seemingly crazy outburst, everyone had been gasping in admiration at the magnificent blue roan. Now Bud Morris couldn't even get a bid of twelve hundred to start the action.

'Come on,' Sandy sighed. She could see what would happen and wanted to get out before Kirstie did too.

The bidding for Moondance would drop lower still, until it fell right through the floor. Then the buyers from the meat markets would step in and offer to buy the mare for peanuts. They would drive her off to the slaughterhouse, and that would be it. A horse with a mean streak was gonna end up as dogmeat, period.

But before Sandy could lead Kirstie and Hadley away, Hadley dug in his heels. 'Where did they say the mare came from?' he checked with Kirstie.

'Aspen Park.' She remembered clearly that this was what Bud Morris had told them. 'That's the spread Ty Turner has just bought.'

Hadley nodded. A deep frown wrinkled his forehead. ' "There ain't no such thing as a mean horse . . ." ' he quoted. ' "Just a mean owner"!'

'Yeah!' Kirstie saw what he meant. 'So why is

Turner getting rid of Moondance instead of trying to solve her problem?'

'Right,' Hadley muttered. He cast one more thoughtful look at the quivering, hard-breathing, defeated blue roan in the centre of the ring. Then he put up his hand to attract Bud Morris's attention.

'I'll pay five hundred dollars for the horse,' he offered in a loud, determined voice. 'Not a single cent more!'

2

'Hadley, I never had you down as a guy with a sentimental streak!' Sandy joked with the old ranch hand during the drive back to Half-Moon Ranch.

He sat up front in the passenger seat, with Kirstie tucked away on a fold-down bench behind. In the back of the trailer she could hear the blue roan mare barging against her stall and kicking at the metal sides.

It had been a tough job loading the horse in the first place. No amount of coaxing and gentle leading had worked. In the end, after forty-five minutes of failure, Hadley and a couple of mounted wranglers from the sale barn had had to use ropes and strong-arm tactics to do the job.

'You goin' soft in your old age?' Sandy teased, easing round a corner on to the five mile dirt track that led to the ranch.

'Nope,' came Hadley's curt reply. 'I bought the mare because I know a good deal when I see one.'

'Aw, come on!' Sandy grinned. 'No one else in the place even put in an offer once they saw the way she was wired!'

'Back off, Mom,' Kirstie muttered. She didn't want Hadley to go and change his mind. 'I reckon five hundred was a neat price.'

'Yeah, a spring blowout sale bargain for a horse of that quality,' Sandy acknowledged. 'But I still say Hadley has this soft centre that he doesn't want anyone to see!'

'Hmm.' Wisely, the old man said nothing more. He just tipped his hat forward and stared out of the window at the steep slopes of ponderosa pines and loose scree.

It was April, and spring came late at an altitude of ten thousand feet. The thorn bushes were still black and spiky, the pale branches of the silvery aspens bare. But the sky was eggshell blue against the white peaks of the Rocky Mountain foothills.

They drove the Shelf-Road in silence, past the salt licks where the cows came for their supply of extra minerals, past the juncture in the track leading off to Aspen Park, until at last the red roofs and green meadows of Half-Moon Ranch came into view.

Home! Kirstie's heart always gave an extra beat when she caught her first glimpse of the ranch house nestled in the trees of the valley. It was a glad, warm feeling to know that she lived in this little patch of paradise.

'We gotta watch how we unload this mare,' Sandy warned, thinking ahead. 'Luckily, Ben has taken the guests on an all-day ride, so we can settle her in before they get back.'

'Yes, ma'am.' Hadley was his normal, uncom-municative self.

'You wanna put her in with the ramuda?' Sandy checked.

'No, ma'am. I'd like to keep her separate in the barn. I'll pay for her feed.'

'Hey, there's no need!' Sandy made it clear that she owed the old wrangler many favours going way back.

'I wanna pay the mare's upkeep,' Hadley insisted stubbornly.

'Yeah well, we'll argue that later.' Sandy eased the trailer under the welcoming ranch sign, down the last steep approach. As she drew up, Kirstie's brother, Matt, strode out of the tack-room to greet them.

'How did we do on the yearlings?' he asked Sandy. 'Did we make a thousand, like we wanted?'

Climbing out of the cab, Sandy nodded. With her fair hair and slim figure, she could have been Matt's older sister rather than his mom. 'We did well. Twelve hundred.'

Matt nodded with satisfaction.

In the back of the trailer, Moondance realised that they'd stopped and she set up a fresh, stormy bout of kicking and barging.

Kirstie saw her brother's expression change. He frowned. Mr Money Man had just jumped to the wrong conclusion.

'So we made twelve hundred on the yearlings,' he grunted. 'But how much did we spend on whatever's in there?'

'This horse didn't cost you nothin',' Hadley cut in before Sandy could explain. 'I came up with the dough myself.'

'You bought a horse?' Matt threw Hadley a puzzled look. He strode to the back of the trailer to take a look inside. 'How come?'

Moondance landed a thump with her back hoof against the rear door. Matt stepped smartly back.

'She's a good horse,' was all Hadley would say by way of explanation. He went to unbolt the door and lead the mare out.

'Yeah, she's a looker, OK,' Matt admitted, though he was still puzzled.

'Hadley won't admit it, but he fell in love with Moondance,' Kirstie told him in a low whisper.

Her voice was drowned out by the violent thumping and kicking from inside the trailer. For a while, Moondance's protests cut short the discussion. The mare had decided that she didn't like being unloaded any more than she'd enjoyed being trailered in the first place. She kicked out at Hadley when he tried to sidle into the box, then set up a shrill, constant neighing which echoed down the valley.

'Jeez!' Matt shook his head as at last Hadley disappeared inside the trailer. 'For a guy who oughta know his way around horses, I reckon the old man has his work cut out with this one.'

'Yeah.' Standing hands on hips in the midday sun, Sandy had to agree. 'But y'know Hadley. He's stubborn as a mule.'

'Yeah, and he's over seventy years old. Most guys

his age move out to Florida and play golf!' Matt decided that Hadley needed help. He ventured on to the tailboard of the trailer, then once more took evasive action as the mare's hooves came flying towards him.

'Easy, girl!' Kirstie could hear the old man's steady voice trying to calm Moondance. 'Use a little savvy, huh? Once we get you outta here and into a nice cool stall, you get water and feed. The full four diamond treatment, OK?'

Something in his voice gradually quietened the frightened horse. And, peering inside, Kirstie could see that Hadley wasn't showing any fear himself. He was moving safely and quietly around the trailer, making her accustomed to his presence. No rush, no force.

And Moondance was beginning to listen. She was flicking her ears towards him, kicking less, not straining so much at her tether. Soon Hadley was actually able to reach out his hand and stroke her beautiful arched neck. But he wasn't looking directly at her, just sidling up to her and running his hand down on to her withers, patting her gently and stroking some more.

'She sure is a looker!' Kirstie whispered.

The blue roan colouring looked like pale mist

in the shadow of the trailer. It swirled over Moondance's broad back and hindquarters, giving her a lighter, more classy look than your everyday sorrel or bay. Plus the white flash on her long face and the white socks on all four feet stood out pure and clear in the semi-dark.

'Hey, and she moves like a dream!' Now that she was calm, Kirstie could appreciate the mare's easy, fluid movement. She turned her neck with perfect grace to nuzzle at Hadley's broad, work-worn hand. And when she shook her head, a ripple ran all the way down her curved, supple spine.

'OK, little lady, time to untie this here rope and lead you outta here,' Hadley said gently, pulling at the slip-knot with practised smoothness. Moondance didn't object. She felt the smallest of tugs on the lead-rope and obediently followed Hadley down the ramp.

'Cool!' Kirstie breathed. And now the mare was super-alert. She took in the yard where the trailer was parked, the ranch house beyond. And on the lower slopes of the valley the newcomer spied the guest cabins and the trails leading through the trees to the mountains beyond. Turning her graceful head, she spied the clear running water of Five Mile Creek; Red Fox Meadow across the wooden footbridge; the towering distant summit of Eagle's Peak.

Kirstie read suspicion in every inch of Moondance's beautiful body. *What is this place? Why am I here?* Head and tail up, snorting fitfully, she peered into the smallest corner for hidden danger.

It's natural, Kirstie told herself. *Any horse with a lick of sense would be on guard right now.* She knew that Moondance would smell the presence of other horses, even though most were out on the trail. And in this new situation, the mare's instinct either to fight or flee would be on full alert.

But that didn't totally explain what she did next.

Something, somewhere, spooked her. Maybe a blue jay spreading its wings and flying off from a nearby cedar. Maybe a click of the latch on the barn door. Who could say? Anyhow, Moondance went crazy again.

She reared and jerked the lead-rope clean out of Hadley's hand. Free of restraint, she kicked and lunged at the trailer, inflicting another dent in its already beaten up silver side. Then she swerved away, towards Sandy, who stood firm, arms outstretched.

'Don't let her cut loose out of the yard!' Hadley yelled, putting himself between Moondance and the wide gate they'd driven through.

The mare charged him, then at the last split second veered off to the left. She kicked up dirt, bucking and writhing in an outburst of anger mixed with deep fear.

'Watch out, Matt!' Kirstie warned. Her brother had turned to try and unhitch a second lead-rope from a nearby fence post. Moondance was about to catch him off-balance and charge past him towards the creek.

Matt turned back fast. Half-blinded by the dazzle and glare of the high sun, he put up a hand to shade his eyes. The lead-rope whipped out towards the

charging horse and the heavy metal clip on one end caught her full in the face.

She squealed and reared, her mane whipping back from her face. There was nothing in her head except the urge to get away from these figures who restrained and beat her with ropes, contained her in dark places and who seemed dead set on breaking her spirit.

'Goddam it!' Matt cried, hurling himself to one side and rolling across the ground.

Moondance landed with her front feet just inches from his head. Then she reared and whirled away, still seeking her means of escape.

So Kirstie sprinted in the only direction the mare hadn't yet tried. She wanted to head her off before she worked out a way past the rails of the corral fence, alongside the barn and out on to open hillside. There was a gate at the end of the barn; Kirstie must shut it, yet there would only be moments before Moondance worked it out. Yep, she'd already set off in pursuit of Kirstie. Her hooves were thudding in the dirt, gaining speed.

Kirstie ran hard. Her hat flew off and bowled against the side of the barn, throwing the mare off course and giving Kirstie precious extra seconds.

She covered the ground to reach the gate, heaved it shut, heard the click, then pressed her body hard against the side of the barn.

Recovering from the distraction of the hat, Moondance came charging at the gate. For a moment Kirstie feared she might either jump it or crash straight through.

But no, another instinct came into play. Moondance judged the gate and saw it was too high to jump. And if she threw herself at it, the chances of serious injury were too high. So at the very last split second, she braced her front legs and slid to a halt.

Beaten. Trapped. At the mercy of the strangers who had bought her.

'There's somethin' about her.' Hadley tried to explain to Kirstie why he'd stepped in to rescue Moondance from the slaughterhouse.

It was early evening. The dude riders had returned with Ben Marsh, the head wrangler, and were right now eating a hearty supper of steak and fries.

Kirstie was out in the barn with Hadley and the blue roan mare. Shadows fell long and cool down the central aisle, and the smell of alfalfa bales stacked to the high roof seemed to create a calm, easy atmosphere.

Hadley leaned on the stall door watching his new mare nip hay from her manger. Still lean and fit after a lifetime in the saddle, nevertheless his face was deeply lined and his eyes looked weary under their craggy brows. 'Don't ask me what it is,' he went on. 'Call it gut feelin'. Or maybe my sense of fair play.'

'How come?' Kirstie was puzzled by this. But she was enjoying the feeling of late sun on her back and the sight of Moondance, settled at last.

Hadley shrugged. 'I look at things this way. You get a mare four years old, like this one here. Ain't a thing wrong with her conformation. Her breedin's pretty darned perfect as far as a working ranch horse goes. It looks like everythin's fair and dandy.'

'Except she bucks and kicks and hits out with no reason.' Kirstie saw what he was getting at.

Hadley shook his head. 'There's always a reason,' he insisted, watching Moonshine intently.

'You don't reckon a horse can be born that way?' Kirstie felt a deep sympathy for what Hadley was saying and pushed him to talk on. 'You know; some horses are just wired wrong?'

'No way.' The old ranch hand didn't raise his

voice, but he was one hundred per cent clear. 'You gotta understand, in the wild a horse is driven by just one thing, and that's the urge to survive. Now, he does that best in a herd because he don't have sharp teeth or claws, or any of the usual stuff that helps an animal to live alone. And a horse is built for speed. Which means that his best tactic when he comes under attack is to run. OK?'

Kirstie nodded. She liked the lazy, laid-back drawl in Hadley's voice when he got into lecturing her about the equine species.

'So, what happens when man comes along, cuts him off from his herd, then puts a halter round his neck and a saddle on his back? Why, naturally he objects. He tries to run and we don't let him. Some of us beat him and kick him and force him down narrow chutes. We tie him up, put a blindfold over his eyes, then get on his back and ride the buck out of him . . .'

'Stop!' Kirstie pleaded. She'd seen for herself some of the cruel old methods used to break a horse. 'And you think Moondance came in for some of that treatment?'

Slowly Hadley nodded. 'It's the only thing I can think of to explain why she's so afraid.'

Kirstie risked a direct look into his lined face. 'So

you did feel sorry for her, like Mom said?'

Hadley grunted. 'Yeah, but I seen a hundred badly-treated horses come through that sale barn in this past winter alone, and I felt sorry for each and every one of 'em. But I didn't buy 'em.'

'So why Moondance?' Kirstie looked at him eagerly, her clear grey eyes shining.

Once more he grunted and shrugged. 'Like I said,' he concluded, standing straight and wiping the palms of his hands on the back of his jeans. He began to walk off down a dust-filled shaft of golden sunlight. 'There's somethin' about her that I just can't explain.'

3

'Everythin's right and everythin's wrong,' was Ben's verdict when he first had a chance to take a look at Moondance.

It was Sunday morning: changeover day at the ranch, when old guests left and new ones got in. The short gap in-between gave the head wrangler a chance to catch up on some office work. But now he'd strolled out of his cubbyhole into the spring sunshine and was watching Hadley's first training session with the unpredictable mare.

'She is beautiful, right?' Kirstie valued Ben's expert opinion.

'Yeah, awful pretty,' he agreed. 'It's that wild mustang look, I guess.'

'But a handful?'

Ben nodded. 'Look how she carries that pretty head, all arched, with her ears flattened. That says "Don't step into my space, mister!" '

They watched in silence for a while, as Hadley drove the mare around the outside of the arena by means of a long rope which he snaked towards her heels to make her move on.

Then, when Moondance seemed to have had enough of the pointless trotting, she let her head drop.

'There you go, that's an act of submission,' Ben pointed out. 'See how she's slowing down to a walk?'

Sure enough, Kirstie saw the blue roan settle into an edgy walk, one ear still turned directly on Hadley as he approached with the rope.

'Most times, that means a horse is ready to parley.' The head wrangler watched for the smallest signs that told him Hadley might be making progress.

'As long as you don't make a sudden move.' Kirstie too recognised the body language. She held her breath as Hadley drew closer.

'Easy, girl,' the old man murmured. 'Ain't no

one here plannin' on sackin' you out or nothin' heavy like that. So let's try bein' nice with one another, huh?' Warily Moondance watched Hadley's approach. With no headcollar or halter rope to restrain her, she could easily take off at a split second's notice.

The muscles in her shoulders quivered, ready for action. Her long, high-carried tail began to flatten tight to her rump. 'Huh!' Ben muttered, ahead of the action he knew was about to occur.

'Yeah, nice and easy,' Hadley coaxed, aiming to get close enough to pet and fuss the mare as a reward for her work around the arena. Quietly he drew in the snaking rope and coiled it in his hand.

Then, *wham!* Moondance hit out. Her spine flexed, her back legs kicked within inches of Hadley's face.

'Close!' Ben said under his breath. 'Good thing the old man still knows how to handle himself!'

Hadley had dodged the hooves just in time. Frowning, he watched the mare flee to the far side of the arena.

Kirstie noted exactly what had happened. It seemed to her that Moondance's crazy actions were starting to form a pattern. The first time, for instance, was when they'd seen her in the sale barn ring. Sure, there was enough going on there to scare even the most laid-back horse – the yells of the auctioneer and bidders, the neighing of other horses in the chute behind, the sea of curious faces. But Kirstie had felt even then that Moondance's bout of madness was linked to the rough way the handler had led her in on the lead-rope.

Then there was the mare's resistance to being led into the trailer. Once inside, she'd been OK, aside from the odd kick and whinny of protest. Then again, she'd hated being led out into the yard when they'd arrived at the ranch.

'You got somethin' on your mind?' Hadley asked her as he walked across to join her and Ben.

'Maybe.' Kirstie needed to think it through. Moondance was nice and calm in the barn, eating her hay. So it wasn't closed-in spaces that got to her. It was something else. Concentrating, Kirstie came up to date with this most recent incident. It had only been when Hadley had approached the mare with the rope in his hand that she'd bucked and kicked. Just like yesterday, after she'd broken free and Matt had tried to get near her with the spare headcollar and the metal clip had caught her in the face. That's when she'd gone totally nuts again.

'Y'know,' she said slowly, watching the cloud of

dust kicked up by the blue roan's loping heels. 'My idea is that it's all linked with the use of lead-ropes and tethers.'

Both Ben and Hadley thought for a while. 'Good thinkin', Kirstie,' Hadley said at last. 'You put your finger on somethin' important.'

Encouraged, she went on. 'Say Moondance has been through some heavy stuff. Whipping and beating, hog-tying, hobbling . . .'

The two professionals nodded their agreement. 'No way would she welcome the sight of a man with a rope after that,' Ben added.

'You reckon I ought to throw away my lead-rope?' Hadley flung the loose coil over a fence post as he put the question. 'Where does that leave me when I want to show her who's boss?'

Kirstie grinned at him. 'Hey, you're the expert. You work it out!'

Hadley smiled. He leaned back against the fence to watch the mare's gait as she passed by. 'Nice trot,' he commented, as if he hadn't just come within inches of serious injury.

Ben looked at his watch. 'Gotta go,' he told them reluctantly.

So it left just Kirstie and Hadley to admire the looks and free flowing action of the unbroken mare.

'It's sure gonna take time,' Hadley admitted. 'But then, time is what I got plenty of.'

Recently retired from full-time work, Hadley had stayed on at the ranch to help out with odd chores. And Kirstie felt that he secretly missed the old buzz of being out all day on horseback, riding the trails with guests or rounding up cattle.

'Can I help you work with Moondance?' Kirstie asked. She'd been dying to get in there ever since Hadley had stuck up his hand and made his bid for the problem mare.

'You bet.' Hadley didn't hesitate. 'How about we fix up a daily arena session for when you get home from school?'

'That's OK by me,' she grinned. 'Working without ropes of any kind?'

'Sure. How are your horse-whispering techniques?' Hadley asked, his voice tinged with irony.

'Huh!' Like Hadley, she'd recently come to believe that the publicity-hungry trainers didn't always live up to their hype. Her train of thought moved quickly on. 'So why did Ty Turner kick Moondance out of Aspen Park if he claims to work with any horse under the sun?' she wanted to know.

' "There ain't no such thing as a mean horse. Only

a mean owner"!' Hadley quoted. 'Yeah, I bin tryin'
to figure that out for myself. You'd think a guy with
his savvy would iron out the kinks in Moondance
himself, rather than send her for dogmeat.'

Kirstie winced at the memory of the blue
roan's narrow escape. 'Maybe Turner inherited
Moondance from Waddie Newton. So he walked in
on a horse that was already out of control.' But still,
that didn't explain the new owner's eagerness to
get rid of her at any price.

'Did I hear you mention the name, Ty Turner?'
Ben popped his head around the door of the tack-
room as Kirstie and Hadley continued to watch
Moondance slow from a trot to a walk. Her flanks
were dark and specked with sweat, her head
hanging low with exhaustion. Hadley went off to
the cold water tap in the yard to bring her a drink
in a bucket.

'Yeah, why?' Kirstie asked Ben, who'd emerged
from the office carrying a letter and wearing a
worried frown.

'I just read through this communication from the
great Mr Turner, and I tell you, I'm lookin' at
trouble!' Ben smacked the paper with the back of
his hand. 'Our new, world-famous neighbour writes
to tell me that it's bad business practice for him to

rent out part of Aspen Park as winter pasture for a rival outfit,' he explained.

'Does it mean we can't send part of our herd up there come fall?' Kirstie checked.

Ben nodded. 'That sends our winter feed bill sky high for starters. And take a look at this.' Roughly pulling a screwed-up coloured pamphlet from his pocket, Ben thrust it under Kirstie's nose.

On the front of the leaflet she saw a photograph of horses grazing in a flower-filled meadow. There was a sprawling ranch house in the middle distance, backed by dramatic mountain peaks. 'Forget the Rest' she read in quaint, western-style lettering. 'Try the Best!'

Inside, she read the spiel about Ty Turner's sprawling 40,000 acres. How Aspen Park offered the genuine cowboy experience plus the modern comforts of hot tubs in every cabin, a heated outdoor pool, a full time chiropractor on hand to ease the aches and pains of a day in the saddle . . .

'That sure makes us look pretty down-home and dowdy, huh?' Ben commented. 'Turn it over and scan the back.'

So Kirstie read on. Under a picture of Ty Turner himself, she took in the fact that the top horse trainer would be resident at the ranch, on hand to run clinics and give private lessons to guests. 'Learn Horsemanship for the Twenty-first Century!' the leaflet concluded. 'Make it Fun. Make it Friendly. Teach your horse the Gentle Turner Way!'

'Kirstie, you gotta watch this!' Lisa insisted, dragging her friend into the ranch house sitting-room.

It was Sunday evening and Lisa had dropped in at Kirstie's place after a visit to her grandpa, Lennie Goodman. Bonnie was in the kitchen chatting with Sandy, and Lisa was waving a video cassette in Kirstie's face.

'I don't want to see a movie of Ty-Big-Shot Turner, thanks.' She was developing an anti-Turner thing, what with the Moondance mystery and the row over winter grazing. So no way would she waste precious time watching the video.

'Hey, lighten up!' Lisa cried, slotting the cassette into the player anyway. 'I brought this movie along specially for you, Kirstie Scott. Even if you don't rate the guy, you'll love the horse, wait and see!'

Kirstie flopped into a deep leather armchair and eased off her boots so that she could curl her legs under her. 'OK, you win. So what's the story here?'

Settling into a cross-legged position by the TV, Lisa explained. 'Firefly is this totally gorgeous wild stallion they found out on the eastern plains of Colorado. He's black from nose to tail, except for one small white star on his forehead. He's your dream horse. Wild and free . . .'

'Don't tell me: Turner shows up and decides he's gonna tame the stallion using his own unique method!' Kirstie had heard it all before. A couple of years earlier, when she was still a little kid, she'd loved to watch beautiful, romantic stuff like this. But now, she'd taken on some of Hadley, Matt and Ben's harder line on the famous horse whisperers.

'Yeah.' Lisa pressed a button and the credits came up on screen. There was a burning sun in the background, a haze of heat across rolling plains, then the silhouette of a wild horse galloping into view. 'And before you say anything else, just promise me you'll watch it through, OK?'

The credits finished and the music swelled. The camera closed in on the horse, picking out the definition of Firefly's muscular body, every detail of his flowing mane and proud head.

Then it switched to a view of a rider on the skyline with the sun behind him. The man sat tall in the saddle, his Appaloosa alert but not moving a muscle. Close to, you could see the outline of Ty Turner's handsome profile.

A slight breeze lifted the Appie's mane. Then, at an unseen command, the horse took off after Firefly. Horse and rider as one pursued the magnificent creature across the windswept plain.

'So?' Lisa had demanded when the movie was finished.

'Neat horse,' Kirstie had admitted. She'd said nothing at all about the trainer though.

Lisa had been disappointed. 'I reckon the guy comes across in a pretty good light,' she'd insisted. 'It takes guts to run down a wild horse, rope him and trailer him. Then, when Turner got him back to Aspen Park, he put in a lot of hours. Firefly was about as angry a horse as I've ever seen, yet Turner proved that his method worked.'

Still Kirstie had refused to admit that she was impressed.

But now, after Bonnie and Lisa had taken off and she was talking it through with Hadley after they'd released Moondance into the arena, she grew more forthcoming about the video.

'What you get to see is a whole lot of Tyler's new spread,' she told the old wrangler. 'New barns, new stalls, new cabins. All looking hunky-dory.'

'You're sayin' that the whole thing is one big ad

for Aspen Park?' Hadley didn't sound surprised. 'So how about Tyler's actual work with the stallion?'

'Pretty good,' Kirstie was forced to admit. 'You see him working Firefly out in the horse's natural habitat. He second guesses a whole lot of stuff about what he'll do next and in the end he corners him down a narrow draw. He ropes him in neat as you like.'

'Hmm.' Hadley made it clear that this was no more than any experienced cowboy would do. 'So what's special?'

Kirstie shrugged. 'Tyler talks it up a whole lot. He says he never uses force, he just reads the body language of the horse. It's a combination of talking, moving quietly, waiting until the moment is right. Then he moves in with a headcollar and rope.'

Hadley listened, then shook his head. 'Danged if I couldn't have made myself a cool million teachin' ignorant city slickers just that!'

This time, Kirstie grinned. 'Yeah. But nice horse,' she repeated. 'As a matter of fact, the best thing about the whole movie was the shots they showed you of Tyler's ramuda. He's got some neat horses on that new spread of his!'

'Hmm. You got the dough, you can soon build yourself a pretty good string.' Making it clear that it was time to get down to work, Hadley swung his leg over the fence and jumped down into the arena.

The action made Moondance pull up sharply, swing around and lope in the opposite direction. No way did she trust the situation, even though there was no sign of a rope.

'Moondance was in the video,' Kirstie recalled. 'She stood out from the rest of the ramuda because of her colouring. And the cameraman zoomed in on her. There she was, looking like butter wouldn't melt!'

'Little do they know!' Hadley gave a wry smile. 'Looks like an angel, acts like a devil.'

As if she knew they were discussing her, Moondance whirled around once again and showed them one of her spectacular bucking kicks. Her nostrils flared wide in angry rebellion. Then with a flick of her white tail, she charged on.

Kirstie admired the spirit, at the same time as feeling afraid. Rather Hadley than her out there in the arena at this moment in time.

'Yeah,' she sighed, considering the job they still had ahead of them. 'Appearances sure can fool you!'

4

'It's weird. Suddenly everyone around here is an expert horse trainer!' Kirstie joked across the breakfast table exactly one week after she and Hadley had begun work with Moondance. Matt had just tried to put her right over what he called 'piggy' mounts like the blue roan mare. 'You gotta be tough,' he'd insisted. 'A horse like that needs to know who's boss.'

'Sure, but tough doesn't mean rough,' had been Sandy's cautionary contribution.

And Ben had come in with the benefit of his experience at his last ranch in Wyoming. 'Over in

Echo Basin we used a special horse-hair bridle that didn't put any pressure on the horse's airway. It's a technique used by the Pueblo Indians way back. You got a problem horse, you should try usin' a bosal.'

Hadley had listened to everyone but not shifted his point of view. 'Time is the only answer,' he'd insisted. 'A lot of time and a whole heap of plain old-fashioned patience to iron out those ingrained kinks.'

'How many times are you ready to get kicked in the plain old-fashioned butt meanwhile?' Matt had asked. He'd cleared his plate, ready for a meeting he'd set up with a website designer who was driving out to the ranch from Renegade.

Hadley had sniffed and shrugged. 'Listen up, sonny. I bin trainin' horses since way back before you were born. I don't even bother to count the little scratch I pick up here and there.'

In fact, Kirstie knew that Hadley had broken just about every bone in his body during his long career. The accidents had left him stiff in some of his joints but not in the least put off from his lifetime fascination with horses. So now she joked Matt and the old man out of a head-on row about how to deal with Moondance. She was looking forward to a Sunday morning session in the arena which

Hadley had promised her, and she didn't want her brother to go around shooting off his mouth and ruffling feathers.

'Anyways, I thought you and Ben had to see a guy about a website,' she pointed out.

Taking a last sip of black coffee before he grabbed his hat, Matt turned to the head wrangler. 'Tell me the name again,' he muttered.

'Will Ryman. He represents an outfit called Ryman Graphics. I ran into him when I was checking out a photographer named Steve Como.'

Kirstie caught the familiar name. 'Isn't he the guy who worked for Ty Turner?'

Ben nodded. 'He directed the movie, 'Firefly'. He also produced the still shots for the Aspen Park brochure. Another branch of Como's business is designing websites, so I reckoned I'd check him out.'

'Sounds like someone we can't afford,' Sandy remarked with a wistful sigh. She had agreed that Half-Moon Ranch needed to enter the twenty-first century by advertising on the internet, but was obviously also worried about the cost.

'Right,' Ben agreed. 'I soon found that out. But as it happens, Will Ryman was on the point of quitting his job with Como and teaming up with his dad. The old guy runs a small graphic design outfit

46

in Renegade. I'm hoping that they'll be more our style.'

'Yeah, well good luck with that,' Sandy said. Then she called after Matt, who was by now out on the porch. 'You remembered I'm driving into Dallas today to watch Brad compete in the State Championship?'

Brad Martin, Sandy's boyfriend, was the current national reining champion. She liked to support him whenever she got the time.

'And you know Lisa is coming here for the day?' Kirstie added. Matt had carried on walking. 'You guys have a nice day,' he called over his shoulder. 'Some of us have got work to do!'

'Who is that totally gorgeous guy?' Lisa sighed as she and Kirstie sat together on the porch swing.

They were gazing out across the yard towards the corral, where Matt and Ben were deep in conversation with a young visitor.

Kirstie sipped her strawberry milkshake. She wasn't concentrating on the three men. Instead, she was on the lookout for Hadley, who had told her he had letters to write and laundry to wash before they could work with Moondance.

'Kirstie, I said, who is that?' Lisa insisted. 'Am I

47

right, didn't we see him in the diner last week?'

Kirstie cast a casual glance towards the corral. 'His name's Will Ryman. He designs websites. We need a website. That's why he's here.'

'And he works for Ty Turner?' Lisa's voice rose to a squeak. 'He's the guy in the pale blue shirt – the one I thought was kinda cute!'

Kirstie looked again, then nodded. 'The same,' she agreed. 'But he didn't work for Turner. It turns out he was with Steve Como, the guy with the camera who came in with Turner later on. And when I say "was", that's past tense, OK? He just quit his job.'

'Pity,' Lisa sighed. 'I wanted you to work me an intro with the guys at Aspen Lodge.'

'You're seriously crazy, you know that?' Kirstie felt disgruntled over her friend's obsession with their new rivals.

'Yeah.' Happy to agree, Lisa stood up from the swing. 'Look, they're through talking business. What d'you say we introduce ourselves to Will anyhow?' Before Kirstie had time to react, Lisa was halfway across the yard.

'Hey, Matt!' she called.

'Hey, Lisa.' Matt smiled back at the high-spirited, irrepressible red-haired girl.

Lisa went right up to the two guys. She fluttered her eyelids and looked meaningfully at Matt.

'Huh? Oh yeah. Lisa Goodman, this is Will Ryman. Will – Lisa.'

'Nice to meet you again,' she gushed. 'I served you breakfast, last Saturday at the End of Trail Diner.'

Talk about up-front! Kirstie said to herself. Subtle definitely wasn't Lisa's style. Even though Will was at least seven or eight years older than them, he was the shy type who might still find Lisa a handful.

'Yeah, sure,' he said slowly, the light of recognition dawning. Taking off his steel-rimmed shades and slipping them into the pocket of his blue checkered shirt, he smiled back. And yeah, he was cute, Kirstie decided. He had the right kind of neat, short haircut, white teeth, a light tan.

'You worked with Ty Turner on "Firefly"?' Lisa rushed on, trapping Will against the fence but allowing Matt and Ben to slide away to do other chores.

'We'll talk about the deal Monday, OK?' Matt called back.

Will nodded. Too polite to escape, he tried to answer Lisa's eager inquiry. 'Steve Como and I worked *for* Mr Turner,' he told her. 'Nobody works *with* him, let's get that straight.'

'Wow!' Lisa was weak at the knees anyway. 'Ty Turner's my hero!' she confided. 'What's he really like.'

Kirstie read more into Will's answering shrug than he was willing to say aloud. 'He's good on camera, I will say that.'

'Jeez, the way he rode down that black stallion!' Lisa sighed. 'I say there ain't a rider in a million that hot in the saddle! And then there was the work he did to break him. It was like magic to watch!'

'Glad you enjoyed the movie,' Will said, obviously ready to change the subject. 'Like I told Ben Marsh, I don't work for Steve Como any more, so I lost touch with the set up at Aspen Park.'

Luckily for Will, this was the moment that Hadley chose to open the gate into the arena and let Moondance enter at a lope.

Kirstie hadn't seen the old man come down from Brown Bear cabin, ready to start work, but she too was glad of the diversion. Sometimes Lisa could be downright embarrassing. 'If you want to see a real expert at work, come and watch Hadley,' she invited Will. Then she turned to Lisa with a remark she couldn't resist. 'Sorry that Hadley ain't as good in front of a camera as Ty Turner!'

Lisa blushed and quietened down.

Meanwhile, Will Ryman was taking in details of the blue roan mare. 'Say, that isn't a horse from Ty Turner's ramuda by any chance?' he asked Kirstie.

'She sure is. Her name's Moondance.' She invited Will to step on to the lowest rung of the fence beside her. 'She'd still be over at Aspen Park when you were shooting the movie.'

'Yeah, I thought I recognised her.' Will's smooth brow had furrowed. He seemed to be thinking things that he wanted to keep to himself.

'Beautiful, huh?' Kirstie prompted.

They watched Moondance lope smoothly around the rim of the arena, with Hadley standing quietly in the middle, apparently doing nothing except turn slowly on the spot.

'She's a looker,' Will agreed.

It was what everyone said when they saw her. 'We worked out that she's got somethin' against lead-ropes,' Kirstie went on, glancing quickly at Will's serious face. What did he know that he wasn't saying?

'Uh-huh. You sure took on a heap of hard work.'

'Hadley did.' Kirstie acknowledged that it had been a week now, and still there was no sign of the mare wanting to make any move towards her new trainers. She would rather wear herself out loping round and round the arena in futile flight than risk going anywhere near either Hadley or Kirstie.

The frown on Will's face had deepened. He was starting to look truly uncomfortable. 'Well, I'm glad she's OK,' he concluded.

Which was a weird thing to say, Kirstie decided. It made her press Will harder for answers to more questions. 'I guess Ty Turner works his staff pretty hard?' she went on, trying hard not to jump down Will's throat. 'I mean, it takes a lot to set up a dude ranch in the amount of time he's taken.'

'You could say that,' Will replied, non-committal as before.

'And he aims to be top dog round here?' Kirstie pressed.

'Yeah, it's in his nature to want to succeed,' he conceded. 'In fact, I never met a man more likely to.'

' "Forget the rest. Try the best!" ' she laughed.

'Corny, huh?' Will managed a smile. 'That was Mr Turner's own idea. In fact, you might say he has a monopoly on having ideas. If you work for him, you put your brain out of gear, or else!'

'Steve Como must have found that hard.' Now

that she'd started Will really talking, Kirstie was eager for him to carry on. 'Didn't he want to use his own ideas when he shot the Firefly movie?'

Will shook his head. 'Steve was happy to take his fee and do as he was told.'

'Is that why you quit?' Kirstie asked.

Will cleared his throat and looked down at the dusty toe of his boot. 'Let's just say I'd rather work with my dad. I'd had a bellyful of guys shooting their mouths off and playing fast and loose with the truth!'

And this was how they left it: Will Ryman angry at the memory of working for Steve Como and Ty Turner, Kirstie more and more curious, Lisa still clinging to her rosy view.

'I guess Will is jealous of Ty's success,' Lisa decided as their visitor drove away.

'Hey, Kirstie, you fixin' to come and do some work, or are you plannin' on standin' round jawin' all mornin'?' Hadley called.

'Coming!' she answered quickly. 'Go check out Ty Turner's website,' she suggested to Lisa. 'Maybe that'll put you back into a good mood!'

So Lisa wandered off into the ranch house while Kirstie climbed the fence into the arena and Hadley clambered out. Moondance noted the switch and loped on.

'Remember, you never look her in the eye,' Hadley instructed. 'That tells the horse you wanna fight her. You just turn around in the centre, maybe watch her legs, her shoulders. That says, "Sure, I'm interested in you. But I'm not about to make the first move." '

'How do you know this works?' Kirstie asked, doing exactly as he said.

'You watch two stranger horses meetin' up in the wild. This is just the way they act. Eventually one gets curious. He lowers his head and comes moseyin' up. Look, it's happenin' with Moondance right now!'

It was true: the blue roan was slowing her pace and lowering her head. She kept on casting glances at Kirstie and her circle grew tighter, drawing in towards the centre where she stood.

Kirstie held her breath. She tried not to alter her body language, but it was hard not to show her excitement at the gradual change in the horse's actions.

'Easy!' Hadley instructed. 'Don't blow it now. This is as close as we got all week.'

Without a rope or halter to help her, taking it

easy was all Kirstie could do. She turned slowly, waiting for curiosity to overcome Moondance. 'Come across when you're ready,' she murmured. 'Just say hi.'

The mare flicked her ears and lowered her head. Her trot became a walk. She stretched out her neck towards the centre of the circle where Kirstie waited.

'Come on, say hi!' Kirstie breathed. 'Make our day!'

Moondance took in every scent and movement. She seemed to pick up even the heartbeat of this stranger who waited for her and whispered gentle words. And she moved in closer.

'Hey!' Kirstie whispered. Still she didn't look the mare in the eye. Instead she stood head down, gaze averted.

The horse edged so near that her muzzle almost brushed Kirstie's arm. She breathed in the smell of the girl, nipped with her teeth at the soft fabric of Kirstie's shirt.

'Yeah, get to know me, check me out.' Holding steady, trying to control her racing pulse, Kirstie felt her excitement rise.

Moondance sidled up to her. Kirstie could sense the heat rising from the mare's body. She smelt her sweet smell, felt her warm breath on her face and hands.

'Jeez, you're a good girl!' Almost in tears, Kirstie raised an arm to the mare's neck.

For a second, Moondance tensed. Then suddenly the fear melted. She accepted the girl's hand on her body, lowered her head and nuzzled the warm palm that stroked her.

'Kirstie took a major step forward with the blue roan,' Hadley told Matt over lunch, giving his apprentice all the credit.

'Yeah?' Kirstie's brother sounded like he still doubted whether taking on the mare had been a good move. Anyway, his head was filled with other things.

'The Rymans are offering a good deal on the Half-Moon website,' he told them. 'Once I talk it through with Mom, I guess we'll go ahead.'

'Tell Will we don't any tacky slogans like "Forget the Rest, blah-blah",' Kirstie reminded him.

Even Lisa had admitted that the Aspen Park site was a little OTT. 'It's like they just discovered dude ranching all by themselves,' she told Matt, Ben, Kirstie and Hadley. 'Whereas we all know that it's been around more than a hundred years.'

'Even longer than me,' Hadley joked.

They all teased him while Matt got up to answer the phone. When he came back, Kirstie could tell straight away that there was a problem. She stopped eating and rattled her fork on to her plate.

'That was Mom,' he began uncertainly.

'Yeah?' Kirstie felt her throat tighten as she looked at Matt's anxious face. Something was definitely wrong.

'She was calling from Denver City Hospital.'

'It's Brad, isn't it?' Kirstie knew that Brad was riding in the reining contest, something he did most weekends of the year. He was national champion, a genius in the saddle. Even so, there was always the chance of a freak accident.

Matt nodded. 'Little Vixen spooked,' he told them. 'Brad ended up under the hooves of another horse. They took him to hospital.'

'How bad is it?' Kirstie whispered. This bolt from the blue made her feel dizzy and sick.

Closing his eyes, Matt shrugged. 'Mom's with him now in the ER,' he explained. 'She says to say a prayer for Brad! Please God that his back doesn't turn out to be broken!'

5

Sandy didn't come home from the hospital that day. The news on Brad was that he was critical, then stable but still in a coma.

'What do they mean when they say his condition is stable?' Kirstie asked Matt. This disaster had put all thoughts of Ty Turner and Aspen Park out of her mind.

'It means they've got all his vital signs under control: his breathing, his heart rate, his blood pressure.' Matt had gained a fair amount of medical knowledge from his training at veterinary school. 'They've hooked him up to monitors and given him a drip-feed to keep his fluid levels up. Now all they can do is wait.'

The information scared Kirstie. She pictured the tubes and screens, their poor mom waiting at Brad's bedside. 'What exactly happened?' she asked Matt as the long day wore on.

He sighed and looked up from the tack he was cleaning as a way of keeping his mind occupied. 'Mom says she didn't see the start of it. All she knows was that Brad was on Little Vixen waiting to come into the arena. A guy called Marty Choo was riding out on Mister Tom. The horse didn't score so well, so Choo was giving him a hard time.

'So they get into the area where Brad's waiting for his turn, and by this time the crowd's yelling at Choo to take it easy on his horse. Little Vixen's uneasy at the noise. Then some idiot lets off a firecracker and there's mayhem. Mister Tom rears up and lands square on Vixen. He hits Brad on the back of the neck on his way down. Vixen spooks, Brad lands in the dirt.'

'Was he already out of it?' Kirstie cut in. The more she heard, the worse the accident sounded.

'Nope. Mom says he must've been conscious because he tried to roll clear of Mister Tom. But the horse was crazy by now. He'd thrown his rider and was stomping around this small area. By the time the wranglers got to him and pulled him out, he'd already stomped on Brad real good.'

Like Sandy had said, they'd better pray hard.

Kirstie left Matt and walked out to the quiet meadow. She needed some space, some time to try and quieten her thumping heart.

Though Brad was a recent feature in all of their lives, he'd already made himself part of the family. Matt had resisted at first, like a lot of grown-up sons do when their mothers set up new relationships.

But Kirstie had liked the brash, gifted horseman from the start. And it was clear that Brad Martin really did make Sandy happy, joking with her and paying her lots of compliments. He had rented a spread near San Luis to train reining horses: near enough to come visit, far enough away not to tread too hard on Matt's toes.

And now he was in the hospital, all wired up and in a coma. 'Please let him get better,' Kirstie murmured, gazing down at the clear running water of Five Mile Creek, then taking a deep breath and glancing up at the mountains.

In Red Fox Meadow the horses grazed quietly, peaceful and rested after their day off. She picked out Lucky, her own beloved palomino, his golden colouring glowing richly in the evening sunlight. Then there was Cadillac, the big creamy-white gelding, alongside Crazy Horse, his constant companion.

'I guess we call a rain check on our session with Moondance this evening?' a quiet voice inquired.

Kirstie turned to see Hadley. He had approached without her noticing and stood in the deep shadow of a tall creek-side boulder. His hat was tipped well forward, his shirt sleeves rolled up to show his sinewy arms and strong wrists.

'Any more news?' Kirstie asked.

'Nope.' The old man's gaze was fixed on the ramuda. 'Y'know, Kirstie, I've bin round horses all my life, and I still have more respect for them than any human bein' I ever met.'

Kirstie felt the same way. It was why she liked to spend time with the old man, though when working he rarely spoke above two or three words at a time. But at times like this he liked to pass on his wisdom. 'What is it about horses?' she prompted him.

'You can count on a horse,' Hadley said after a long pause.

'Yeah,' she agreed. 'But I can trust some people too – my mom, for instance.'

'Sure, you're lucky. I didn't have none of that

when I was a kid.' Without taking his gaze off the peaceful herd, Hadley went ahead and shared some of his life story.

'I was born in Idaho, but my folks passed away before I was five years old. I went to Wyoming and was brought up by an aunt, my mom's sister. She and I didn't get on, so by the age of fifteen I quit school and I was working for a big outfit called Harrison Land and Cattle. I was livin' the cowboy life, ropin' steers and brandin' them, part of the great cattle drives across the western plains.'

Kirstie listened hard. It was the first she'd ever heard of this. 'That must've been tough.'

'Nope. Like I said, I learned to like my own company. Then I had a good boss by the name of Abigail Harrison. She gave me a hundred opportunities that most kids my age never dreamed of. By the time I was twenty-two I was the youngest foreman in the state of Wyoming. The way that lady looked after me and treated me makes me want to cry remembering it.'

'But you still don't put her above the horses you worked with?' Moved by Hadley's account, Kirstie pushed for more information.

'Pretty near,' he admitted, grinning briefly. 'Mrs Harrison made me see that if you want somethin' enough, you can get it, but that you don't have to step on other people on the way. I got that lesson learnt, and I never had any reason to change my mind about it.'

'Hadley, tell me Brad is gonna be OK,' Kirstie whispered, feeling closer to him than ever before. Like a little kid, she wanted him to give her the happy ending.

'I can't do that,' he said quietly.

'But you said if you want something enough you can make it happen.'

'I mean the things that come under your control, like the job you do, the way you behave. But this don't come into that category. This one ain't down to us.'

Kirstie knew it really. She sighed and looked up at the red sun sinking towards the mountains.

'So we call off the training session until tomorrow?' Hadley went back to his original question, wanting a reply.

She frowned and gave herself a small shake. 'No way,' she said. 'We work with that blue roan, come rain or shine!'

'Hard work pays off,' Hadley insisted. 'There ain't no magic way of gainin' a horse's trust.'

It was something else that Kirstie knew deep within herself. No instant solutions. Just perseverence.

Through Monday, Tuesday and Wednesday, she and the old man carried out their training programme with Moondance.

As news came through from the hospital that Brad was out of the coma but was still unble to move or speak, everyone at Half-Moon Ranch concentrated on the routine tasks without Sandy to lead them.

'I need to be here,' she told Kirstie over the phone on the Thursday evening.

Kirstie had called her after school from San Luis. She was in the Goodmans' apartment above the End of Trail Diner, waiting for Hadley to show up in his battered pick-up and give her a ride home.

'Sure, Mom, we understand. And you don't need to worry; me and Matt can take care of things.'

Kirstie ran through the guest list with her, kept her up to date with the new website, told her that they'd brought Hadley out of cosy retirement to help full time.

'And how's that blue roan mare?' Sandy asked. 'Did you get a saddle on her yet?'

'Nope. But she joins up great now,' Kirstie

reported. 'We set her loose in the arena and she comes to me of her own free will. I can handle her and fuss her just fine.'

'Good job, Kirstie. And did Hadley put her out in the meadow with the other horses, or is she still in the barn?'

'In the barn. He says she's not ready to join the others. Too many lead-ropes and headcollars around the place.'

Sandy listened, glad to have her mind on things other than Brad for a few moments. 'Hadley knows his way around,' she murmured. 'You learn all you can, you hear?'

'Yes ma'am. And you tell Brad we're thinking of him all the time.'

'Sure thing, honey.' Sandy's voice grew low and husky. 'You take care of you, huh?'

'Likewise.' Kirstie hung up with a big lump in her throat, to find Lisa watching her with a concerned expression.

'You OK?' Lisa asked. 'D'you want a hot chocolate with mallows?'

Kirstie forced a smile. 'No, thanks. How about we clear tables for your mom?' Anything to keep busy while she waited.

So they went downstairs to a full diner and started

cleaning up after departing customers.

'Am I seeing things?' Bonnie joked from behind the counter. 'Or did I really see my teenaged daughter volunteer to do some work?'

'Very funny,' Lisa retorted. She was about to return some smart remark when the door opened and her face broke into a welcoming smile instead. 'Hey, Will!' she called across the room, smoothing her unruly hair and going out to meet the new customer.

Will Ryman grinned back. 'Thought I'd drop by to pick up a cup of the best coffee this side of Dallas,' he flattered, smiling too at Kirstie and Bonnie. Then he sat down at a corner table.

'How's things?' Bonnie called, putting the coffee to boil.

'Good.' Will looked tired but happy, and as cute as ever. Today he wore a neat business shirt and chinos, but the usual trendy shades adorned his handsome face. 'I finally persuaded Kirstie's brother to go ahead with my design for the website. Man, does he drive a hard bargain!'

'Don't tell me!' Kirstie agreed. 'Matt is the original miser!'

'He's OK,' Will shrugged, taking the coffee from Lisa. He invited the two girls to sit and talk a while.

'I can do business with a guy like Matt because I know where he's coming from.'

Lisa had already grabbed a seat and pulled it up to Will's table when Bonnie spotted her move to get out of work. 'Hey!' she warned. 'These tables don't clear themselves!'

With a groan Lisa stood up and offered the seat to Kirstie. More customers were coming in. 'Mom sure knows how to play on my guilty conscience!' she grinned, shoving Kirstie into the chair. 'Talk websites!' she ordered under her breath. 'Talk about anything you like, so long as you keep him here until I get through with the dishes.'

Kirstie sat down awkwardly, suspecting that Will Ryman didn't really want to waste his time on her.

'How's Moondance?' he asked.

'She's doing great.' She blushed then recalled the strange remark that Will had made when he visited the ranch. 'What did you mean, you were glad she was OK?'

Will stirred sugar into his coffee. 'Yeah, I've been thinking about that,' he admitted. 'It must have sounded pretty strange.'

'There was something you weren't telling me,' Kirstie guessed, sensing the same hesitation as before. 'It's OK, I won't pass it on. I was just figuring it could be useful to know what had happened to make you say that.'

'You're right. I guess I owe it to you guys.'

'Not to us; to the horse,' Kirstie pointed out. 'So why *wouldn't* Moondance be OK?'

Will took off his sunglasses and looked directly at her. 'This is between you and me?'

She nodded, ignoring the noise and bustle of the diner, focusing only on what Will Ryman was about to tell her.

'Because the situation between me and Ty Turner is already bad,' he warned. 'And I don't want it to get out that I told you any of this.'

Once more Kirstie promised.

'OK, so this goes against all the stuff that Turner puts out about his Gentle Training Technique. I was working on the Firefly movie at the time, remember, and I wasn't happy with things I saw at Aspen Park.'

'Such as?' Kirstie prompted.

'Such as the type of guy Turner hires to work with the horses. Some of them don't know zilch about ranch work. They treat horses like pieces of machinery. Anyways, that wasn't the biggest problem. I pretty soon picked up the idea that Turner himself says one thing and does another.'

Kirstie took a sharp intake of breath. 'How does this involve Moondance?'

'I'm getting to that. I'd noticed the blue roan from the start. She was a mare that Turner took on when he bought the spread. He wanted us to feature her in the movie because she's got this wild mustang look.

'Only, it turned out Moondance didn't want to be a movie star. And she didn't seem too happy about being handled by Turner.

'One day she objects to the rope he's lassoed around her neck. She tugs free and I guess Turner thinks that shows him up in a bad light, especially since we're shooting at the time. So he totally loses it with the mare. He grabs the end of the rope with the metal clip and he raises it over her. He brings it down hard, right into her face. Once, twice, three times, with the film crew standing by helpless.

' "Cut!" Turner yells at us. "Stop the damn camera!" He keeps right on beating the horse across the face and neck. The metal clip is cutting into her flesh . . .'

'Hold it!' Kirstie whispered. She felt sick to the stomach. 'Didn't anyone move in to tell him to stop?'

Will frowned. 'You don't tell Ty Turner to do anything!' he insisted. 'Unless you want to lose your job on the spot. I don't feel good about that, believe me.'

'But now you quit of your own free will,' Kirstie pointed out. 'Why not come clean about what you know?'

Will looked even more uneasy. 'Turner's a powerful guy,' he reminded her. 'That's all I'm saying.'

Kirstie nodded and went back to the scene Will had described. 'Did Turner call the vet for Moondance after he'd finished beating her up?'

'Nope. He told one of the guys to treat the cuts with anti-septic cream and keep an eye on her. As soon as the cuts were healed, he wanted her sent straight off to the sale barn; no reserve price, no nothing. He just didn't want to hear another word about her.'

'Jeez!' Kirstie thought of all the high-minded stuff that Turner put out in his brochure and in the movie. 'Listen, how come he wanted to feature Moondance in the first place? I thought the idea was for him to fly his team out to Eastern Colorado and track down an untamed mustang?'

Will allowed himself a shallow laugh. 'Yeah, the black stallion. Or should that be "stallions"?'

Kirstie gasped. 'You mean, Firefly isn't one single horse?'

Will shook his head. 'We used four separate horses to make that movie,' he admitted. 'And not one of them had even seen the plains of Colorado until Turner shipped them out there!'

'Fake!' Kirstie was so angry that she forgot her promise to keep Will Ryman's account a secret between himself and her. She was sitting beside Hadley on the drive home, practically boiling with fury. 'Ty Turner is a fake from start to finish!'

Hadley stared at the road in silence. He took in every word she said.

'He beat up Moondance with a lead-rope!' she told him. 'So we were right about that. No wonder she goes crazy every time she sees one. On top of that, the guy set up the whole Firefly thing on a lie. There was no wild stallion. Never, ever! Just a bunch of identical horses that Turner had picked up at sale barns around the country.'

Still Hadley said nothing. But his eyes narrowed and he clenched his lean jaw. He swerved to avoid three mule deer that sprang out of the bushes and dashed across the Shelf-Road.

'You know in the movie when you see him sitting

on the ridge at sunset, watching the wild mustang race across the plain? That was all fake. So was the running him down into a narrow draw. All they did was trailer a horse in there and have Turner throw a lasso over his head. Will says camera tricks and special effects did the rest. And you know something? One of those stallions actually had to be destroyed! They filmed him running too close to a slickrock because that was the shot Turner said he wanted. The horse lost his footing and slid down the rock, broke a leg and they had to destroy him right there at the bottom of the cliff.'

'Yeah, I bet they didn't keep that bit in the movie

either,' Hadley grunted. 'You let me know something like this and I wanna go right over there to Aspen Park and tell the guy straight: if he goes on mouthin' lies and fakin' it to earn himself a heap of dough, I'll stand up and yell it from the top of Eagle's Peak – "Ty Turner is trash! The guy ain't fit to clean my boots!" '

'No, don't do that!' Kirstie swung round in her seat. 'You're not supposed to know anything about it. I promised Will . . .'

Hadley swung down the drive into the yard at Half-Moon Ranch. He raised a cloud of dust, jumping right out of the car with a grim look as he came round and leaned through the window on Kirstie's side.

'You leave it with me,' he told her firmly. 'I tell you, when I think of Moondance and the way she is because of how she was beat, it drives me crazy. Ty Turner may be famous and powerful and mean as they come, but no way is he gonna get away with this!'

·

6

Kirstie had never seen Hadley so angry. All Friday evening he'd been on the point of carrying out his promise to go and confront Turner head-on.

'Think about it,' Kirstie had argued. 'Where does that get us? We only have Will Ryman's word against the great Ty Turner. Who are people gonna believe?'

Hadley had accepted what she said. 'But it would sure make me feel better if I gave that low-down rattlesnake a piece of my mind!' he'd muttered.

They'd worked together with Moondance, probably more determined than ever to pull her round from the deep trauma she'd suffered at Aspen Park.

The mare was by now in the routine of coming out into the arena at sunset, and she'd shown more signs that she was willing to parley with the old man and the fair-haired girl. She'd even come up to Kirstie and nuzzled her hand when Kirstie had had a lead-rope tied around her waist, only stopping to sniff at the rope and make sure that it wasn't about to do her any harm. Then she'd walked placidly alongside her, taking nips at the handfuls of grain that Kirstie had scooped out of her jacket pocket.

And the progress they'd made had calmed Hadley down some. Still, he'd muttered under his breath all the time they were returning Moondance to her stall and bedding her down for the night.

'That cheatin', lyin' son of a gun!' he'd drawled, tossing fresh alfalfa into the manger. 'If we could put the finger on him, it'd make my . . . whole year!'

Which was how come Kirstie was driving alongside Hadley in his old pick-up on the Saturday morning. They were heading for Denver and Steve Como's city centre office.

Matt had waved them off at dawn, telling them to take care. 'No hothead stuff,' he'd warned Kirstie.

75

'If you wanna talk to the guy to see if he's willing to hand over the movie footage – fine. But don't try to force his hand, OK?'

Kirstie had promised to take it easy. It had been her idea, but Hadley had grabbed at it with both hands.

She'd gone up to Brown Bear cabin late at night to find the old man sitting on his porch swing in the moonlight. 'I've been thinking,' she began.

Hadley had made room on the swing and listened hard.

'Will Ryman told me the cameras were rolling when Turner started to beat up Moondance,' she told him. 'So it figures that the original tape contains all the evidence we need.'

Hadley had nodded and guessed her plan. 'We talk to the director, huh?'

'Yeah. His name's Steve Como. He's based in Denver; I looked him up in the phone book. How about it?'

She hadn't even finished her sentence before Hadley had fixed a time to visit.

And now they were snarled up in the city traffic, having put in a phone call to Como-Vision Enterprises from an out of town gas station. Como had been surprised by the call, but had agreed to see them at nine-thirty.

'I guess I should've scrubbed up a little,' Hadley muttered, glancing in the overhead mirror at his grey stubble. In Denver, his black, broad-brimmed stetson and dusty cowboy boots would make him stand out a mile.

'Then again, I figure havin' a shave ain't gonna make a whole heap of difference.'

They pulled off a main street between tall tower blocks, waiting at lights and weaving through slow-moving vehicles until they came to the parking lot which Como had described to them over the phone. Minutes later, they were hovering in the reception of a smart office suite.

Kirstie recognised straight away the medium height, trim, grey-haired man who came out of an inner room to greet them. Minus his heavy camera and bag of tricks which he'd had with him in Bonnie's diner the first time she saw him, he came across as well dressed and perhaps overly conscious of the way he looked.

'Mr Crane?' he said guardedly, taking in the old wrangler's faded work clothes. He nodded at Kirstie, but said nothing.

'Sir,' Hadley began. He held his hat by the brim

and turned it awkwardly as he spoke. 'We've come to ask about the movie you made for Ty Turner out at Aspen Park.'

'Yeah, that's what you told me on the phone.' Steve Como sounded impatient. 'So go ahead; ask.'

'We picked up a piece of information a couple of days back. It ain't so much the official movie we're interested in as the stuff that ended up on the cuttin' room floor.'

Kirstie saw Como's expression harden.

'What kind of stuff are we talking about?' he asked.

Hadley cleared his throat and pushed on. 'We hear there was an incident involvin' a blue roan mare that wouldn't be included in the official video that Turner released. But we figure you'd still have the uncut version stashed away and we were kinda hoping—'

'You figured wrong,' Como cut in. 'I trashed everything we didn't use. And anyways, I don't know who you've been talking to. I was there one hundred per cent of the time, and I don't remember any incident with a blue roan.'

'It don't matter where we got our information,' Hadley said steadily. 'Let's just say it's important to us to find some hard evidence . . .'

'Against Ty Turner?' Como made sure he understood. 'Oh, come on, Mr Crane, this isn't making any sense. What kind of incident are we talking about here?'

'I got a mare over at Half-Moon Ranch, just outside San Luis,' Hadley explained, coolly holding Como's gaze. 'Now I picked her up at the sale barn for a rock bottom price. It turns out she came from Turner's spread and she's a horse with a history that Turner didn't reveal.

'What I'm saying, Mr Como, is she came to me with a bad problem in that she won't respond to a headcollar and lead-rope. Believe me, that problem is down to Turner, and you have the evidence we need to prove it.'

Just like Hadley to give it to Steve Como straight, Kirstie thought. She was trying to work the movie maker out, but his eyes were growing more and more guarded and his mouth had set in a grim, downturned line.

He smiled at Hadley without meaning it. 'Someone's been telling you lies, Mr Crane. And my guess is it would be Will Ryman.'

Hadley stayed silent. No way would he implicate anyone.

'Yeah, Will Ryman,' Como concluded anyway.

'That's the type of trick a punk like that would pull. Especially after I told him to quit his job here.'

'I happen to believe what we were told,' Hadley insisted. 'Besides, I got a gut feelin' that Turner is suckin' in a whole lot of simple-minded folk who need to be put straight about what he can and can't do with a problem horse.'

'Yeah, well, I'm sorry I can't help you there.' Como shook his head and got ready to show them out.

He's rattled, Kirstie thought. *He's trying to blame Will just to throw us off the scent. Now he's uptight and wanting to get rid of us.* Not for a moment did she believe the movie director's denials.

But he had steered them out of the door and into the elevator before they knew it.

Hadley looked at the red arrow descending to the ground floor and sniffed. It expressed all he needed to say on the subject of Steve Como.

'I guess we'd better think of another way to nail Turner,' Kirstie sighed.

It was frustrating, knowing that there was the movie evidence that would show him up to be the cruel cheat that he was. But they had to face facts: so far they hadn't progressed an inch in their mission to knock a big hole through big-shot Turner's Forget-the-Rest, We're-the-Best image.

While they were in Denver, they called in at the hospital to check in with Sandy and ask after Brad.

It was the first time Kirstie had seen her mom in a week, and she found her looking tired and pale but trying to put on a brave face.

'Brad's able to speak a little now,' she reported. They sat together in a small room beside the Intensive Care Unit. 'He even told me a joke earlier today!'

Kirstie smiled. 'Was it a good joke?'

'No, it was really bad.' Sandy smiled back, then let a sigh escape. 'It's driving him crazy not being able to even lift his head, let alone sit up and walk around.'

'What do the doctors say?' Kirstie asked.

'That there's still too much swelling around the spinal cord to be able to say if the damage is permanent. That horse sure kicked him bad though.' Sandy was warning Kirstie and Hadley not to expect too much when they went in to see the patient. It was just as well, because Kirstie still had to hold back a gasp of dismay when they went into the unit.

Brad was surrounded by monitors and hooked up to drips. Only his face and shoulders were visible above the white sheet. He rolled his eyes towards the door when they entered. 'Not a pretty sight,' he apologised.

Closer too, Kirstie saw that his face was purple and swollen, his right eye half closed. 'Jeez, Brad!' she whispered. She left it to Hadley to try and carry on a half-way normal conversation.

'You got someone to take care of Little Vixen while you're in here?' he inquired, setting his hat down on the clean white sheets.

'My cousin came up from Colorado Springs. Hey, Hadley. Sandy tells me they brought you out of retirement?'

'Hmm.' He gave the familiar dismissive sniff. 'Yeah and my old bones don't take it so good any more,' he confided. 'You just get yourself back on your feet, you hear? We need the boss back at the ranch, so I can go and sit on my porch swing full-time!'

'I'll see what I can do,' Brad grinned through cracked lips. 'From what I also hear, you've gone soft in your old age!'

Hadley grunted. 'You talkin' about me and the blue roan?'

82

'Yeah. How come you took on a handful? It ain't like you.'

'She's a good-lookin' mare,' came the defensive reply. 'Mind you, she does have a problem.'

Kirstie grinned at her mom. It was good to get Brad talking about his favourite topic. As she heard Hadley launch into the subject of Ty Turner, she too filled Sandy in on the latest events.

Sandy nodded and offered an opinion. 'I'm not certain Hadley should go making an enemy of a guy like Turner,' she said in an undertone. 'No way do I want open season between them and us. We have to live peaceably as neighbours, whatever we happen to think of him in private.'

Kirstie agreed, telling her that she'd managed to dissuade him from driving right on over to Aspen Park to give the boss there a piece of his mind. 'Leave Hadley to me,' she murmured. 'I'll keep his attention fixed on making progress with Moondance, so he doesn't have time to go making unannounced visits at Aspen Park!'

'Good!' Sandy nodded.

'. . . Yeah well, good luck with the blue roan,' Brad was saying to the old wrangler. 'If there's anyone who can get her back on the rails, it'd be you and Kirstie!'

* * *

After the short visit to the hospital, Kirstie and Hadley hightailed it back to Half-Moon Ranch in time for Hadley to lead a group of dude guests on their final ride of the week. But first Kirstie gave Matt and Ben a good report on Brad's progress. 'Mom says, think positive!' she told them.

Ben had split the guests into three: beginners, intermediates and advanced. Each group was due to head out of the corral in a different direction, depending on the degree of difficulty the wranglers judged they could manage. After a week of riding, everyone was looking relaxed and maybe just a little bit sad that this was to be their last expedition.

'You take care of Moondance, you hear?' Hadley gave Kirstie a strict instruction. 'You're gonna be the only one around this afternoon, so it's down to you to look in on her every now and then.'

'No problem!' she assured him with a grin. 'Honest, Hadley, you're worse than a mother hen!' Secretly, she was looking forward to a few hours mooching round the barn and the tack-room with no one to bother her.

So she waved everyone off and hummed as she went into the tack-room, fetching a cloth to wipe the blackboard and write out afresh the list of new guests and horses which Ben had already lined up for the following week. She noted that the list was growing longer as the season got underway, in spite of the new competition they were facing from Aspen Park. Maybe they would have no need to worry after all.

Still humming and singing a snatch of a cowboy song, she finished her task then strode off across the corral.

Time to look in on the blue roan, as Hadley was so fond of calling Moondance. Kirstie smiled to herself at this. Who was he trying to fool, refusing to call Moondance by her name? 'The blue roan' – as if she was just any old horse. Really, he was totally gone on her, and everyone knew it. Still, if he wanted to keep up the pretence . . .

'Hey, Moondance!' she called softly as she walked down the central aisle of the barn.

The mare looked over her stall door and watched quietly.

'You glad to see me?'

Moondance reached out with her long, sinuous neck to nibble at Kirstie's empty palm.

'You thought I'd brought you something nice to eat, huh?' Giving up on the search for food, the horse nudged Kirstie's shoulder, then let her run her hand down her soft grey cheek.

'You think I'm crazy, talking to you like this?' Kirstie laughed. 'Most folks do. But I tell them, "This little lady understands every word I say!" Don't you agree? You're smarter than the average human, believe me!'

The soft tone seemed to fascinate Moondance. Her deep brown eyes gazed at Kirstie's smiling face, and she kept on ducking her head to ask for more attention.

'You're terrific, you know that?' Kirstie murmured, loving the one-to-one. Then it came into her head that the bond between the two of them might now be strong enough for her to work in the stall on the very thing that still lurked as a dark shadow at the back of Moondance's mind.

'Wait here,' she ordered, knowing full well that the horse had nowhere to go. She strode off to the far end of the barn, took a halter and lead-rope from a hook and swiftly returned. Moondance pricked up her ears and eyed the suspicious rope.

'It's OK, this isn't gonna hurt. This here is a halter.' Kirstie showed her the collar and let her sniff cautiously at it. 'And this is the rope to fix through the metal loop. Lucky and Cadillac, in fact all of the other guys don't object to wearing it because it means we can easily lead them in from Red Fox Meadow to have a good feed and what have you.'

Moondance looked at her and listened. She inspected the soft, frayed rope with interest.

'Good girl!' Kirstie praised her for not backing off. She wondered if she should risk buckling the headcollar around Moondance's neck to get her used to the feel. But then she decided to give it a rest and come back later. 'See!' she told her, taking away the rope and collar and hanging them on the hook. 'No problem!'

She was back in the tack-room, sweeping the floor with a stiff broom. Dust was coming up in thick clouds and making her cough.

'Jeez!' she spluttered, blaming Ben and Matt. 'Look what happens when Mom's away! Those guys don't do any housekeeping!'

Clattering the broom into hidden corners and reaching under the long rows of saddle hooks, Kirstie at first ignored a sound from outside. She held her breath and went on sweeping.

But it came again – the sound of a car engine, plus the high squeak of brakes. Then she heard Moondance whinny from the barn.

Weird! she thought. How could a car approach the ranch along the creek? Yet that was definitely the way it had come; down a dirt track through the forest, avoiding the official entrance and the drive.

Really weird! To do that, the visitor must have used a back road in, probably one of the Forest Rangers' Jeep trails. But it would have had to cut through razor wire to come over on to Half-Moon Ranch land. Or maybe the fence was down, and that was what the car driver had come down to tell them. She'd better go out and deal with it.

Putting down the broom and shaking the dust from her hair, Kirstie stepped out on to the tack-room porch. Sure enough, there was a white saloon parked at the far end of the barn. But as far as she could see, no driver.

'Hi there!' she called, heading for the car.

From inside the barn, Moondance began to kick up a storm. She whinnied and squealed, then kicked out at the sides of her stall.

Jeez, didn't the stranger know any better than to go upsetting their mare? Kirstie frowned. OK, so he might think the whole place was deserted, but anyone with his head screwed on would surely go to the house and knock on the door before he started investigating inside the barn.

There were more wild cries from Moondance and a sudden click inside Kirstie's head. No way was this normal. The visitor must have heard her calling him and deliberately ignored her. Which meant he was creeping about without permission and spooking their horse.

She stood uncertainly by the car. Should she call again? Or should she creep in after the unwanted guest?

Choosing the second option, she decided on a novel entrance. If she climbed the stack of hay bales from this side, she could get into the barn and take a good look at the stranger from up high. But she'd better be quick; Moondance was going crazy.

So she climbed the bales and slithered on her stomach across the top of the stack, just in time to see a shadowy figure do something unbelievable.

It was a tall, thin guy and he was crouched close to Moondance's stall. The horse was rearing and flailing with her hooves, whipping back her head and squealing with fear. The intruder reached up a hand to grab the bolt which held the stall door in place. He slid it back with a loud metallic scrape. Then he flung the door open wide.

'Hey, don't do that!' Kirstie yelled, leaping up

and launching herself down the bales towards the aisle.

The man spun round and saw her tumbling towards him on an avalanche of hay. Kirstie got a good view of his face before he turned and ran.

Moondance reared and cried out.

Kirstie reached the ground, flung herself at the door and closed it before the horse had time to bolt.

Then she ran into the open, after the crazy guy who had just tried to set their blue roan free.

7

The intruder had reached his car by the time Kirstie made it outside. No way was she gonna catch him before he hightailed it out. In any case, he was tall, strong and fit – someone she ought not to tangle with.

Wait a second! Kirstie stopped dead. Surely she'd seen the guy some place before. But where?

As he ducked his head to get into the driver's seat, he caught his hat against the door arch and knocked it to the ground. The hat rolled away in the wind. It gave Kirstie a good look at his face: long, with a square jaw and drawn, tired-looking cheeks.

Yeah: Bonnie's diner! A week ago this same guy had been eating breakfast there! He was the one whose legs went on forever, who was moaning long and loud about never getting a day off.

Kirstie watched him slam the car door, turn the key and lurch forward. He turned the car around on two wheels with a squeal of tyres. Then he headed out the way he'd come.

Frowning deeply, she went and picked up the dusty hat. This really sucked. And it only half made sense.

The long-legged guy worked for Ty Turner. Which meant that he must have been acting on Turner's orders when he cut through the razor wire and drove his car down the back trail to the ranch. Turner must have targeted Moondance in some way and have a bad intention towards the beautiful blue roan. But why?

Walking slowly back into the barn, Kirstie tried to figure it out. Moondance was hard evidence of Turner being a fake. Therefore he might want to get rid of her in case it ever came to an open confrontation. But how would he know that she and Hadley were on to him?

Back in the cool shadows of the barn, Kirstie stood and stared at Moondance. The mare was gradually settling in her stall after the sudden intrusion, but still restlessly tossing her head and swishing her tail.

Jeez, of course! Kirstie got it in a flash. *The visit to Como-Vision!* Steve Como had been pretty hostile, denying everything, telling them he'd trashed the out-takes from the Firefly movie. But they hadn't believed him for a moment. No; Como had been covering for Turner. So what would he do as soon as Kirstie and Hadley had left the building but get on the phone to Aspen Park and speak with the 'boss'!

She felt her heart sink into her boots. She pictured Como warning Ty Turner that they were on to him, that his whole horse training business, even the dude ranch he'd just set up, would be under threat if the news about him beating up Moondance got out. Turner would've gone crazy at the news. And his first knee-jerk reaction had been to send out one of his hands to kidnap the 'evidence'.

But no – not kidnap. The intruder would have needed to bring along a trailer to do that. So it was something else.

Maybe it would be enough just to set the blue roan free, she thought now, approaching Moondance and sliding into the stall beside her.

She reached out and stroked the arched neck. The horse responded by ducking her proud head and nuzzling close.

If the guy had figured the ranch was deserted this afternoon, then all he would have had to do was slide the bolt on the stall door and let Moondance run.

An empty stall. A mystery disappearance. No clues. That would've been the perfect solution.

And meanwhile, the abused horse would have taken to the hills and run for miles. There was no fence out there that could keep her in. No men with cruel ropes. Just miles of forest and mountain in which to hide.

That Saturday afternoon felt like the longest Kirstie could ever remember.

For the first half hour after Turner's man had driven off, she didn't dare to leave Moondance's side.

Of course, he would be crazy to come back and try again, now that he knew she was home. On the other hand, maybe having to face Turner's anger would make him take the risk. So she listened to every sound, expecting the worst.

Then, when she'd convinced herself that there

would be no second attempt and that Moondance was safe, Kirstie figured out the pros and cons of calling her mom in Denver.

Normally, yes; Sandy would want to know what was taking place. Her calm, cool way of thinking would soon come up with a solution.

But not now, when Brad was still dangerously ill. This Moondance problem would just add to her burden. And Kirstie began to feel that since Hadley and she had got into the mess, it was up to them to get themselves out. So the best way through was to wait until Hadley got back from his trail-ride.

But there was one phone call that Kirstie felt she should make.

'Hi, Will?' She'd run over to the house and rapidly dialled the number.

Will Ryman answered casually, off-duty and relaxed. 'Hey. Who's that?'

'It's me, Kirstie Scott. From Half-Moon Ranch, remember?'

'Sure.' Will immediately grew more alert. 'How's the blue roan?'

'Moondance is fine. But that's why I'm calling you.' Kirstie paused, then plunged on. 'Listen, Will, I owe you an apology. I opened my big mouth and spilled the beans to Hadley Crane about Turner's treatment of her. I'm so sorry. It just kinda spilled out without me thinking.'

There was silence from the other end of the phone.

'Are you still there, Will?'

'Yeah. Did you tell him the rest, about Turner faking the Firefly story?' By now, Will Ryman's voice was uptight.

Kirstie confessed that she had. 'And there's worse,' she admitted. 'Hadley and I had this idea that we could get some film footage out of Steve Como as evidence of what Turner had done to Moondance.'

This time there was an audible intake of breath. 'Oh great!' Will moaned. 'Didn't I mention that Steve is married to Turner's sister? He's part of the Ty Turner dynasty!'

Kirstie groaned. 'No, you didn't. And he guessed that you were our source of information, Will. Hadley refused to admit it, but Steve figured it out anyway.'

'Which leaves me, you and the old man in the firing-line.' Will saw where it left him. 'Not to mention the blue roan.'

'And still no evidence,' Kirstie pointed out. 'Como said he trashed all the spare footage.'

'That's true; he did.' Will sounded thoughtful. Then he said something that made Kirstie's flesh creep. 'You remember I said to keep all this stuff under your hat?'

'Yeah,' she admitted.

'That was because you don't ever stand up to Turner and survive the experience in one piece,' he warned her. 'The guy's power mad, and on top of that he's a control freak. When we were filming at his place I once saw him horsewhip a ranch hand who stepped in to question a decision of his. The guy speaks out and Turner reaches for the whip and beats him senseless.'

'Like he did with Moondance?'

'Yeah; animal, human – it makes no difference. And it was in front of witnesses. But you know something? Not one of us who saw what happened reported it to the cops. The reason being that not only did Turner pay our salaries, but his personality is the kind that grabs you by the throat and half chokes the life out of you. So we all ended up turning our backs once we'd treated the poor guy's cuts and bruises. We said no way would we stand up in court and describe what happened; we were all way too scared of Turner.'

Kirstie felt the hand that held the phone begin

97

to shake. 'OK, I get the picture,' she told Will. 'What will you do now?'

'Lie low – maybe move out of my parents' place for a while and stay with a friend. Hope that Turner has bigger fish to fry and that he'll forget about me. As a matter of fact, Kirstie, I advise you and Hadley to do the same.'

'You mean back off from taking this Moondance thing any further?'

'Right. And find some way of letting Turner's people know that you've decided to drop it.' Will doled out the advice in a strained, urgent voice. 'Otherwise he's gonna turn and run you, your mom and the whole Half-Moon Ranch outfit clean out of the state!'

Kirstie watched Hadley lead his group of dude riders down Bear Hunt Trail.

She could pick him out from a distance, sitting stooped in the saddle, hat low over his forehead, riding as if he and his bay horse were one. Rodeo Rocky, moving along in a jog trot, respected every small shift of weight, tug of the reins or tap of the spurred heels that Hadley used to guide him with.

Don't tell him. Don't say a word! Kirstie repeated

the last instructions she'd given herself as the group descended the steep slope.

She knew she was between a rock and a hard place; that whatever action she took now would have its downside.

On the one hand, she could tell Hadley about the mystery intruder and the conversation she'd had with Will Ryman. *But imagine that*, she'd told herself as she'd worked the rest of the afternoon in the barn and kept Moondance within her sights. Hadley wouldn't even wait until she'd told him the whole thing through. No, he would explode with anger against Turner. This would be one step too far. He would drop everything and drive straight across to Aspen Park, have a head-on clash with Ty Turner, and Kirstie wouldn't be able to stop him.

On the other hand, she could try to keep the whole incident to herself. As soon as things had calmed down, she could work out a way of getting through to Aspen Park and explaining that she and Hadley had made a big mistake and that she now realised that Turner was everything he claimed to be. Grovelling would be tough, but it might be for the best.

But this would demand real nerve on her part. She would have to steel herself not to say anything, to act as if things were normal and take on all the decisions herself.

Yet this was what she had decided in the end. Sure, it meant Ty Turner would get away scot-free yet again. And yeah, it was the coward's way out. But, scared as she was, Kirstie figured that it gave her and Hadley their best chance of keeping Moondance safe at Half-Moon Ranch.

'Hey!' Hadley greeted her as he rode Rodeo Rocky into the corral. 'How's the blue roan doin'?'

'Fine!' Kirstie told him, moving in to help riders dismount and unsaddle their horses.

There was a mood of quiet satisfaction amongst the group of advanced riders. They'd ridden their last trail, stayed in the saddle over difficult terrain and now had to say goodbye to their faithful pals.

So Kirstie kept busy, carrying the heavy saddles into the tack-room, briskly avoiding the sad farewells.

Then she had to lead the tired mounts to Five Mile Creek, water them and release them into Red Fox Meadow. By the time she'd finished this, Matt and Ben's groups had also returned. So it was almost suppertime before she had any more conversation with Hadley.

'You been tryin' to avoid me?' the old man quizzed

as she stepped out of the tack-room on to the porch. He was studying the new list of horses and riders that would come into effect next week.

'No way!' The answer came out too sharp and pat.

'You sure you ain't got nothin' to report on the roan?' Hadley gave her a shrewd look. 'She ain't been kicking up a storm or nothin'?'

'No. Why?' Kirstie followed him across the corral into the barn.

'I noticed a couple of cuts on her front leg, that's all.'

Nothing escaped his eagle eye. So Kirstie had to think fast. 'Oh yeah, I guess I did hear her spook at something while you were out. I was in the middle of sweeping out the tack-room. By the time I got over here, Moondance had calmed down again. I didn't think anything of it.'

Hadley opened the stall door for a closer look at Moondance's small injuries. He seemed to accept the excuse Kirstie had given him, calling for a barrier cream to apply to the cuts before they led the horse out for her evening training session.

But Kirstie felt awful. There was a knot in her stomach over the lie she'd just repeated. It screwed her insides up tight and made her feel sick. Maybe it was the wrong decision. Maybe she should tell Hadley everything.

But when she returned with the cream, the old man was ready to get down to business.

'Tonight we try putting a headcollar on her,' he told Kirstie, working quietly inside the stall. 'I figure she's ready for it.'

Kirstie agreed. 'I let her take a good look at one earlier this afternoon and she didn't even tense up.'

'Then you go ahead,' the old wrangler invited, stepping to one side. 'The plan is to buckle the collar on in here and lead her out to the arena, OK?'

Nodding, Kirstie fetched the equipment. She found that the challenge hardened her shaky nerves and made her concentrate on the immediate task. So it was a case of easing into the stall with the rope already attached to the collar, of talking quietly and reassuringly, of letting the mare sniff at the coarse nylon webbing of the headcollar.

'Easy, girl,' Kirstie breathed. 'You've seen this before, remember? Yeah, this is what we do, see? We slip it over your nose nice and smooth. There's a small fastener that buckles up just so.'

Moondance took a small sideways step as Kirstie fixed the headcollar in place. When she found herself restrained by a lead-rope, she tugged her head and looked puzzled.

'Hey, quit pulling!' Kirstie coaxed in the same low, gentle voice. 'You must remember all this stuff from way back. It didn't hurt then and it's not gonna hurt now.'

'OK, try leading her out,' Hadley advised, easing open the door. 'But remember, if she cuts up rough, you jump clear!'

She nodded. No way did she want twelve hundred pounds of angry horse rearing up and crashing down on her in the narrow confines of the barn. At the first sign of trouble she was ready to jump.

But, as it turned out, they needn't have been afraid. Moondance felt Kirstie's hold on the lead-rope tighten and she followed, meek as a lamb. Straight down the centre aisle, beneath the towering stack of hay bales, out through the wide door into the corral, she walked without protest.

'Good job!' Hadley called from behind.

Kirstie's heartbeat quickened. With Moondance at her shoulder, they wove their way through the rough wooden tethering poles towards the open arena. Their problem blue roan mare, the horse with the crazy streak who had been destined to become dogmeat, was good as gold!

Wow, was she proud! Here Moondance was, walking quietly at her side, round and round the arena. Kirstie changed direction. The horse followed. She stopped. She started again. 'Hey, Hadley!' she called, wanting the old man to witness this small miracle.

There was no answer, so she walked Moondance around the arena to the point closest to the barn door. As they arrived, she saw Hadley walk out carrying a dusty black stetson.

Kirstie stiffened. It was the hat that had fallen from the intruder's head as he made his getaway. She must have forgotten to clear it out of sight after

she'd picked it up and Hadley had stumbled across it.

'Where did this come from?' he asked sharply, turning the stetson around between his hands, trying to see if it was one he recognised.

'Search me!' Kirstie shot back. She felt her face burn red with shame. She'd had a second chance to tell the old man the truth and once more she'd deliberately chosen not to. 'I've never seen it before.'

'Huh!' Hadley sounded upset. He didn't like strange hats turning up out of nowhere. It disturbed his sense of order and made his hackles rise.

'Maybe it belongs to one of the guests,' Kirstie suggested, her heart in her throat as she led Moondance round the arena.

'It don't look like a dude hat,' Hadley grumbled, throwing it down on a nearby bench. 'To me it looks like a real cowboy's hat. But if it ain't mine, nor Ben's, nor Matt's, then who in darnation does it belong to?'

The mystery of the hat remained unsolved. Hadley had asked around in vain. The stetson was left lying on the bench where he'd thrown it down.

And Kirstie went to bed that night with a storm

of emotions whirling inside her. First was the hot-and-cold guilt she felt about deceiving Hadley. Even if it was for a good reason, the act of lying was to her a shameful thing. Not that she didn't kid and fool around and fib like everyone else. But she didn't tell big, barefaced lies. It had made her queasy, sent her to bed early, almost straight away after she and the old man had finished their most successful training session to date.

Then there was fear. What if she couldn't get through to Ty Turner? Say he couldn't be convinced that the people at Half-Moon Ranch weren't launching a campaign to expose him? Will Ryman had laid it on the line for her – Turner was a monster who could turn violent for reasons much less important than the one she and Hadley were giving him.

If Kirstie had felt cold and shivery when she thought of deceiving Hadley, now, when she pictured Turner's temper, she felt ice run through her veins.

She lay awake long into the night, staring out of the window at the stars and moon, listening to the coyotes howl up on Bear Hunt Overlook.

Then when she slept, her dreams were vivid. She saw Moondance out under the night sky, her mane silvery white in the darkness, her dappled coat ghostly. The tall trees cast black, flickering shadows that spooked the horse and made her flee. Kirstie was in her own dream, standing watching the blue roan gallop along the ridge and over the horizon.

She set off at a run to catch the horse. But something tied her to the spot. She ran without moving an inch, growing breathless and desperate. Moondance had already disappeared, her hoofbeats were fading, Kirstie would never see her again.

And the thing that was preventing her from moving was a lead-rope tied fast around her ankle. Kirstie stooped to untie it and found the knot impossibly complicated. She pulled and tugged, wore a rope burn into her skin, listening in vain for the hoofbeats . . .

Kirstie woke up suddenly in a pale grey dawn. Her face was covered in sweat, she was breathing uneasily.

She was awake and still something was wrong. Badly wrong.

She slid out of bed and into her clothes. Within seconds, she was downstairs and out of the house. The thing that was wrong was somehow linked with her dream. Which meant that it involved Moondance. Fear held her in its icy grip.

Kirstie began to run. She crossed the yard and came within sight of the barn. The door hung open wide. Anything – bears, coyotes, mountain lions – could have crept inside.

And the whole place was quiet. Too quiet. There should have been a rustle of straw from Moondance's stall. The mare should be awake, alert to the sound of footsteps approaching. Yet there was nothing.

With a dry throat and a thumping heart, Kirstie reached the stall.

A second door stood open.

Kirstie held on to the doorpost for support. She looked again to make sure she hadn't still been dreaming the first time. There was straw strewn everywhere, a plank kicked out of the manger, other signs of a struggle.

But there was no blue roan mare huddled in a corner, waiting for Kirstie to come and calm her.

Empty. Kirstie closed her eyes. *Empty*.

Which meant that Turner's men had returned in the dead of night and finally carried out their cruel plan.

8

Kirstie's first thought was that Moondance was dead. They'd crept in under cover of darkness and put an end to their problem. No horse: no evidence of Turner's crimes against her.

She stepped back and sat down weakly on a hay bale. The knowledge that she'd made the wrong choice fell like a hard blow. It winded her and made her bend forward to catch her breath.

This was all her fault. She should have come clean with Hadley and asked for advice. Now the blue roan was dead because of her terrible mistake . . .

Get a grip! she told herself. Figure it out. No way

could Turner's men have committed the deed on the spot, or even in the neighbourhood of Half-Moon Ranch. So if they did plan to murder Moondance, they would've had to trailer her out to a secret place, probably in Aspen Park territory.

Which gave Kirstie a small breathing space. It was an hour's drive from here to Aspen Park, maybe longer in a trailer. Supposing that real-life sounds from the barn was what had woken her from her nightmare; that would mean the criminals still had practically the whole drive ahead of them. She had sixty short minutes to come up with a rescue plan. But her brain was spinning and the clear thinking she needed wouldn't take shape.

'You gonna tell me what's goin' on?' a voice said.

It made Kirstie jerk to her feet like a puppet on a string. 'Hadley!'

He stood in the centre aisle, staring into the empty stall.

'What are you doing here?' she demanded. It was six in the morning. The dawn mist hadn't cleared.

'I woke with a bad feelin'. Now I know why.' Taking a few steps towards her, Hadley fixed Kirstie in his gaze. He didn't say anything else, he just waited.

'Hadley, I'm sorry!' Guilt made her stumble over

the words that gushed out of her mouth. 'I screwed up. Turner sent a guy out here yesterday afternoon. I hid it from you because I thought I could handle it. Now it turns out they came back and took Moondance!'

The old man nodded. His thin lips were set in a grim line, his eyes narrowed so that Kirstie couldn't read what was going on inside his head. 'Save it,' he muttered. 'Ain't no time for "sorry". We got some figurin' to do!'

'What will they do to Moondance?' Kirstie hung on tight to the door strap as Hadley threw his old pick-up around a sharp bend on the Shelf-Road.

The grey mist still clung to the hollows of the steep banks and swirled around the high tops of the ponderosa pines. Hadley's vision was limited to around twenty yards on the twisting road ahead.

'You're askin' me a question I can't answer,' he muttered, gripping the steering-wheel and swerving to stay on the track.

They'd figured it through back there in the barn and come up with a few cold certainties.

For starters, Moondance's disappearance was definitely down to Ty Turner. No way could the mare have escaped unaided. Neither could it have been an attack by a bear or a mountain lion, since there was no sign of blood shed during the struggle that had taken place.

So Turner's guys had come back. But did they just set the mare loose? Hadley had wanted to check this one out thoroughly. He'd sent Kirstie one way around the outside of the barn to pick up possible tracks. Taking the other side himself, they'd met up around the back.

'Did you find anythin'?' he'd asked. 'Any recent hoofprints in the dirt?'

She'd shaken her head, then Hadley had led her a few yards towards the creek and pointed out fresh tyre tracks. The marks had indicated a long, heavy vehicle, coming down a back trail, stopping, turning and driving out the way it had come.

And there had been enough scuff marks where it had parked to guess that a horse had been led into it.

So that had been the proof they'd needed. And once they'd made certain that this was what had happened, Hadley had leaped into action.

He'd ordered Kirstie to jump into his pick-up without even giving her the time to tell Matt what was happening. 'No one's awake yet. I'll radio them once we're on the road,' he'd promised.

And that was it – six-fifteen on a Sunday morning, and they were in a race to save the blue roan's life.

'Do you reckon they'll shoot her?' As she clung on hard and was flung this way and that by Hadley's reckless driving, Kirstie couldn't stop the dreadful images from flooding in.

'I guess,' the old man replied, grimmer than ever.

She could see this would be the cleanest, surest way. And now, as they sped out on to the highway, she wondered if Hadley had chosen the right route. He'd deliberately avoided setting off along the back trail in direct pursuit of the trailer. Instead, he'd figured on using the fast, smooth main road to arrive at Aspen Park even before the horse thieves made it back. Then they'd be in place to confront Turner with what he'd done.

But had that been a good guess? Would the ranch hands drive the trailer all the way back to the house? Or would they stop off on the way, get out their guns and shoot Moondance dead?

'Maybe we should turn around!' she gasped, explaining why. 'Let's try and pick up their trail instead!'

Hadley shook his head. 'Those guys don't do nothin' without direct orders from the top,' he told her. 'Turner's the man we gotta confront.'

So they sped on, past still-sleeping gas stations and quiet roadside houses, along empty stretches of white road until they came to a turn-off for Aspen Park.

Kirstie noted the bright new sign that Turner had had painted. It told drivers that the ranch was three miles down the track, offering a four diamond welcome to dude guests and weekly clinics for problem horses. She glowered, then stared straight ahead, preparing herself for what lay at the end of the narrow road.

Hadley wasn't the type to pussyfoot. He knew Turner's reputation, yet he drove right on up to the ranch house at ten after seven on a Sunday morning and pulled up with a squeal of brakes alongside a brand new black Jeep.

The big house was new, but built out of logs in the old pioneer style. Three storeys high, with smart shutters and a tall stone chimney stack, it dominated the smaller guest cabins spread out behind. Over the main door Kirstie spotted a huge pair of moose antlers, and on the long porch was a cane rocking-chair tipping gently back and forth as if someone had just vacated it.

But there was not a soul in sight. Following

Hadley's example, she got out of the pick-up and took a good look around.

Turner had changed and improved the old Waddie Newton spread almost beyond recognition. Close to the house he'd built a new round-pen for clinic work. Beyond that was an open arena some sixty or seventy yards in diameter. And there was a covered area for schooling attached to a huge barn – everything that a professional horse trainer would need.

Hadley came alongside her and nudged her with his elbow. 'Take a look at the bunkhouse,' he suggested. 'But make it seem like you're not noticin' anythin' special.'

Kirstie took a sly look at the low, simple row of wooden cabins where Turner's men hung out. She spotted a half-open door and a slight movement of the blind at one of the windows. 'We're being spied on!' she whispered.

Before they had time to react, however, they heard the front door of the main house open and saw Ty Turner stride out.

He was as Kirstie recalled, both from the brief encounter in Bonnie's diner and from the famous Firefly movie. In other words, he was careful to make an impact in his immaculate jeans, his crisp blue shirt and his newly brushed white stetson. Standing on the porch, thumbs hooked into his belt, a big chunk of gold glinting on his finger, he eyed his unexpected visitors.

'I came for the blue roan.' Hadley spoke right out.

Behind his back, Kirstie held her breath. This was exactly what she'd known he would do, and the very thing Will Ryman had warned against. Yet, now that things had gone this far, what else could they do?

Turner came down the two steps from his porch. He spoke in a voice filled with scorn. 'Go home, old man!'

Hadley didn't back off even a fraction of an inch. 'Not until you hand over my horse.'

'I don't have your horse.' About to shrug and turn insolently away, Turner was stopped in his tracks by Hadley's next remark.

'Sure you do. You sent your guys over to Half-Moon Ranch and trailered her out. They were under orders to drive straight back here on the forest road. I picked up their tracks where they rejoined the highway a mile before your turning.'

His words made Kirstie clench her fists. Hadley hadn't mentioned this last part to her as they drove in at breakneck speed. It meant that the ranch hands had beaten them to it and that Moondance was already here, hidden away somewhere on Turner's luxurious spread.

The big boss's sudden hesitation turned into a long pause as he realised how much Hadley had guessed. Then he slipped into arrogant denial. 'I don't know what's going on inside that addled head of yours,' he protested. 'Maybe you've been out in the sun too long, huh? All I know is I sent a blue roan mare to the sale barn because she was surplus to requirements – no other reason.'

Hadley's stare grew steely. He didn't interrupt as the lies and sickening excuses poured out of Turner's mouth.

'What happens? I get a lousy price for the mare, then I forget all about her. The next thing I know, I hear you're the new owner and you're snooping around, spreading lies and blackening my name. Now here you are, the man himself, giving me the evil eye and talking garbage when you should know better.' Turner levelled his gaze to fire the parting shot. 'Like I said before, get along home, old man. Go ease your aching bones on a cosy porch swing.'

Kirstie saw that it had become too much for Hadley to bear. He cussed under his breath and strode to within two feet of Turner. 'You lay one finger on that blue roan and I swear I'll kill you. You hear me?'

'I hear you threatening me,' Turner answered with a dismissive laugh. He looked over Hadley's shoulder towards the bunkhouse and gave a prearranged signal for two of his ranch hands to come running.

Seeing them, Kirstie backed away and slipped behind Hadley's pick-up out of sight.

The men covered the ground fast. Hadley heard and swung round to face them, leaving himself open to Turner from behind, who charged the old man and sent him sprawling forward into the dust.

Hadley hit the deck face down, rolled and scrambled up in time for the first of the two wranglers to land a punch direct to his stomach.

Three against one. Cowering behind the pick-up, Kirstie searched in the back for something she could use in Hadley's defence – a crowbar, a mallet – anything.

But then she heard Turner give the next order.

'Hold it!' he told the two wranglers. 'We don't want to cut him up too bad. That would look like we went over the top when the sheriff arrives to throw him off ranch property for trespassing.'

Reluctantly they left off punching their victim

and instead pinned his arms behind his back while Turner went inside the house to make his phone call to Larry Francini.

'Count yourself lucky, old man!' the first hand muttered. He was the tall, gaunt intruder who had driven out to Half-Moon Ranch the day before. 'If it was down to me, no way would you be standin' on two feet right now.'

The other twisted Hadley's arm up his back until Hadley was forced to squirm with pain.

And it was then that Kirstie hit on a new plan. OK, so Hadley was in trouble, but Turner had already let slip what he planned to do with him. There was to be no more violence, presumably because, short of outright murder, it was too risky. With Hadley alive but badly beaten, then Sheriff Francini and the rest of the San Luis County Police Department would be asking Turner some serious questions. So for the time being, he had to take it easy and Hadley was safe.

Now, if Kirstie managed to slip away without being seen, she could grab the chance to carry on with the search for Moondance. It would only be a minute or two at most until Turner or his men realised that she was missing. But please God, that would be enough.

Perhaps recognising what Kirstie might be planning, Hadley took it on himself to give Turner's wranglers as much trouble as he could. He started to struggle free, kicking out and using all his strength to break their grasp.

The two men held on, breathing hard and swearing.

It was now or never. Kirstie judged the distance between herself and the nearest object behind which she could hide. It was the six-foot-high palisade fencing, surrounding the round pen. Beyond that was another open space, then a side entrance into the barn, which was where she wanted to be. If she made it to the palisade without being seen, she felt she could probably work her way there and take a good look around.

So while Hadley fought back, she crouched and ran fast as she could for the fence. Twenty yards felt like a mile, ten seconds like an hour.

But she made it without a rough voice calling her back or the sound of feet crunching across the dirt after her.

For a split second she leaned against the far side of the fence to draw breath. She blew out through her cheeks, ducked low then ran on. Five seconds later, she was inside the vast barn.

She closed her eyes in relief. But time was ticking by. Turner would have made his call to the sheriff, he would be coming back out of the house and looking round to see where she was. And she must find Moondance before he found her.

As her eyes grew used to the dark, she saw with a sudden start that her luck might be in. There, parked at the far end of the barn, was a small silver trailer, just the kind that Turner's men might have used to transport the stolen mare.

She raced towards it, praying that there had been no time for the thieves to unload.

But the trailer was empty. Peering inside, Kirstie saw evidence: soiled straw, a lead-rope dangling from a hook. But no Moondance. *So close, yet not close enough.*

Where had they put her? Might it be in the long row of stalls down the side of the barn? For the first time, Kirstie stopped to listen for clues. And she heard what she was hoping for – a shuffling and a low snort – signs that at least one of the stalls was occupied.

Her heart in her mouth, she hurried towards the noise. Out in the yard, voices were raised. She heard Turner yell an order for one of his men to go look for her. OK, so she probably had only seconds left.

But she was approaching the stall, hearing louder kicks and clicks of hooves against the hard floor, then a suspicious whinny.

Sprinting now, she drew level with the horse inside the stall.

He was pure black with a white star. He pranced and snorted inside his small space like a wild beast. Pure mustang, hating his captivity.

'Firefly!' Kirstie breathed. She felt herself choke with disappointment.

The famous stallion lifted his head and squealed angrily.

Footsteps began to run towards the barn. Kirstie stumbled on towards the next stall and leaned for a moment against the door. There was a slight sound from inside, the outline of a second horse caught in the low glare of the rising sun shining through the side of the barn.

Kirstie blinked and looked again. The poor creature hung its head, its sides heaving, tethered on a short rope to the far wall. It shook and flinched at the sores covering its body, tried to draw away from Kirstie, then sank on to its knees.

And now there was no mistake. Kirstie made out the beaten, bruised form of Moondance in the shaft of pale sunlight. The blue roan stared back at her with helpless, pleading eyes.

Finally the footsteps entered the barn. Turner's man was framed in the doorway.

Wasting no time, Kirstie flung open the door and seized the rope which held the blue roan prisoner. She slipped the knot, vaulted on to the horse's bare back and, whispering in her ear, quickly urged her out of the narrow stall.

9

Kirstie rode Moondance straight at the wrangler. He stood his ground until the last possible moment, legs apart, arms spread wide. Crushing him against the door post, the horse surged by.

Without a saddle, Kirstie felt the power of the blue roan's stride. She had only the long, white mane to cling to and her own skill as a rider to rely on.

And now they'd hit the full glare of the daylight and could make out the second wrangler then Turner himself standing in stunned surprise. Hadley had wrenched free and was running towards his pick-up.

'Ride her out of here up on to that ridge!' he yelled. 'I'll meet you there!'

By a shift of weight and pressure from her leg, Kirstie managed to turn Moondance in the direction Hadley was pointing. She saw a hill rising steeply to the horizon, thickly covered with aspen trees and scattered with granite boulders. The ground beneath was loose dirt, sage scrub and thorn bushes. Not easy territory to cover bareback, especially on such a highly-strung horse.

Yet Moondance saw the challenge and flew at it, churning up grit as she hit the lowest part of the slope before she reached the trees. Her hooves thudded into the soft ground and slid back, so that for every three steps she took forward, she lost one in the downslide.

By this time, Turner and his two men had got over their shock. There was a lot of shouting, opening and then slamming of car doors, then the sound of two engines starting one after the other.

Glancing round as Moondance made progress up the hill, Kirstie saw Hadley's pick-up roar out of the yard on a dirt track that cut across the valley bottom then turned left through a clearing in the trees. There would be a point about half a mile along the ridge where Hadley's path would join with hers.

But that was only if Turner let Hadley get that far.

She saw the black Jeep that had been parked by the ranch house close on the pick-up's tail, riding fender to fender as if playing some crazy game of chicken. Turner himself was at the wheel, with only one of his wranglers. Glancing quickly over her shoulder, Kirstie soon spotted the reason – the familiar thin guy was following her on foot.

'C'mon, Moondance!' Kirstie urged the mare up the hill. She ducked under low branches and leaned to avoid the slender silver trunks as they gained height towards the ridge.

'Good girl!' she murmured, clinging tight to her mane and trying to make her body as one with the swaying, straining, swerving horse.

Way over to the right, Hadley's car had reached the turn-off up the hill. He took it at speed on only two wheels, in a cloud of dust and dirt that spat up into Turner's windscreen and sent the ranch owner careering off-road into a gulley.

Kirstie saw that the near-accident had given Hadley precious extra seconds. Now there was a real chance that they could meet up to work out the next step in the plan.

'Yeah, we made it!' she breathed as Moondance reached the solid granite rock that topped the tree-covered slope. Two hundred yards below, her own pursuer still scrambled after them.

Breathing hard, the horse stopped dead on the ridge, and for a few seconds, Kirstie couldn't work out why. 'C'mon!' She coaxed her gently over the sliprock, kicking her heels against Moondance's sides.

They edged forward until they crested the top of the ridge to feel the soft warmth of the rising sun on their faces. It was only then, in the deceptive gentle glow, that Kirstie realised why the horse had suddenly resisted.

There was a sheer drop on the far side. The rock fell away vertically for some fifty or sixty feet, until it reached a fast-flowing creek half hidden by more boulders and trees. Spectacular at the best of times, the sight now made Kirstie feel sick and dizzy.

'OK, I got you!' she whispered to her horse. Suddenly she wished with all her heart that they were tacked up with saddle and bridle, since riding this ridge bareback felt like crossing the Niagara Falls on a tight-rope.

Gingerly she eased Moondance back from the summit, cutting down to the safety of the soft dirt and then beginning again to traverse the hill, towards the spot where she was to join up with Hadley.

If he made it! Once more she caught sight of the car chase between the trees. Hadley was still ahead, but the Jeep had dug itself out of the gulley and was making up ground fast. Kirstie saw its square grille flash in the sunlight and its thick, tough tyres eat up the ground which Hadley's old pick-up struggled over. Within seconds, Turner was hot on his heels again, bumping his fender in an effort to drive Hadley clean off the trail.

Kirstie was still easing Moondance along the hillside just short of the rocky ridge. But now a different fear entered her head.

What if Hadley *didn't* make it? That left Kirstie and Moondance face to face with Turner and trapped from behind by the guy on foot. So maybe it wasn't such a good idea to meet up as planned. With only a couple of hundred yards to go, it still might be safer to turn right around and head in the opposite direction. Then they could make a clean getaway. Maybe Hadley had even registered this at the start and yelled the order to meet up as a clever decoy?

Then again, turning around would mean leaving him at Turner's mercy. And that guy was so cruel and arrogant he might easily force Hadley into a head-on crash with a giant boulder.

Confused and afraid, Kirstie stopped to consider.

The engines of the two cars screamed and whined up the hill. Hadley's pick-up hit a bump and flew through the air, landing with the scrape of metal against rock. It gave Turner time to draw level and start to nudge Hadley sideways off the track. Hadley fought for control as his pick-up tipped at a steep angle, two wheels in the gulley.

Kirstie practically stopped breathing. *Enough!* she thought. *Please give in, Hadley, before you get yourself killed!*

But it was against the old man's nature to admit defeat. And besides, it was Moondance's life that was also at stake. So he fought with the steering-wheel to get back on the track and stay ahead of Turner. With another crunch of metal he made it and raced on up the hill.

That meant Kirstie had to see this through too. No way could she desert Hadley when he was prepared to risk his own life for the blue roan.

Besides, the guy chasing her had watched her hesitate and must have seen what was in her mind. He'd changed course and was taking a direct route to cut her off from any retreat along the ridge. What was more, he was carrying a gun.

A cold shock ran through Kirstie when she saw the weapon. It was snug and solid in his hand, aimed at her from a distance of fifty yards.

'Hold it right there!' the man cried. 'Don't make another move until the boss arrives!'

Kirstie froze. Moondance felt the sudden tension in her body and went into super-alert stance, ears cocked, tail flattened ready to run.

'Easy!' Kirstie breathed. A girl on a horse was an easy target for a man with a gun at fifty yards.

And by now, Turner's Jeep was making one last charge up the hill after Hadley. The pick-up was almost at the ridge and the black four-wheel drive was pushing to the limit.

Almost closing her eyes, Kirstie looked through a blur of lids and eyelashes. Did Hadley know he was heading for a sheer drop?

He drove with his foot full down on the pedal, engine screaming, wheels churning up dirt.

'Stop!' Kirstie pleaded, forgetting about the gun pointing at her, even unaware by now of the threat that still hung over Moondance.

As Hadley reached the ridge, Turner suddenly braked and steered off to one side. He left Hadley to drive on, straight over the sheer cliff edge.

But the old man's reactions were quick. He crested the ridge and saw the deathly drop, slammed on his brakes and slewed the wheel hard around. The car spun on the last ten yards of rock, its back end teetering on the very edge. Then Hadley opened the door and rolled out sideways. Free of his weight, the pick-up rocked backwards, slid on its long metal belly until it was tilted beyond recall.

Kirstie saw it rock and finally go. For a split second the whole thing looked strangely graceful, as if filmed in slow motion. Then it dropped, back end first. With the sound of shattering glass and crunching steel, it disappeared over the edge.

'Pity,' Turner sneered. He'd had his co-passenger in the Jeep go and drag Hadley to his feet then pin him against the nearest rock. Then, as the car vanished, he'd pulled a gun from his own pocket.

Now, having ordered Kirstie, Moondance and her pursuer to come close, he obviously felt he could afford a short breathing space.

'Yeah, it's a pity you didn't go over the edge with the truck,' he commented, staring coldly at Hadley. 'That would've been kinda neat – no nasty bullets for the cops to dig out of the corpse. Just pure accident.'

'You want me dead, you gotta come up with somethin' better than that,' Hadley drawled, playing for time. He didn't look like a man who'd just stared death in the face. 'So what's it gonna be? *Two* bullets, *two* corpses found on Aspen Park land? Ain't Sheriff Francini gonna find that a mite suspicious?'

Mention of the law jerked Turner into fresh action. Without changing his aim, he turned his head towards Kirstie. 'Get down from that horse,' he snapped. 'And do it fast!'

'Right!' Hadley challenged loudly before Kirstie could move. 'Talkin' of the sheriff, didn't you make a phone call? Ain't he on his way out here?'

A worried look came over Turner's confident features. Not exactly panic, but a realisation that things weren't all going his way. Swiftly he crossed to where Hadley stood.

'Get this!' he muttered, shoving his gun into the old man's ribs. 'Either you tell the girl to get down from the horse and hand it over, or I make a hole in you as big as the Grand Canyon!'

'Yeah, and what then?' Hadley held up his head and answered back. 'Your guys get a rope around the blue roan's neck and spook the heck out of her all over again? You set it up so she's out of control and all you can do is put a bullet in her head. End of story!'

Turner nodded. 'Something like that. I got witnesses to back me.'

'And, contrariwise you got me and Kirstie!' Hadley reminded him.

'Yeah.' Turner was back to his old sneering style. 'But you're the guy who bought a horse from me and it turns out you can't do nothing with her, remember? You're pretty mad, so you try to bring her back as faulty goods.

'You want your money, I say a deal's a deal. You bear grudges, so you try inventing wild stories about car chases and guns to blacken my good name. There ain't a grain of truth in it; that's how it's gonna look.'

'So what do we gain by doin' as you say?' Hadley challenged. 'If we hand over the blue roan, she ends up dead.'

'If you don't, *you* end up the same way.' Turner seemed to grow tired of arguing, so he hardened his line. 'Say you and the girl were in the car when it went over the edge. They find your bodies all smashed up beside the wreck. My guys tell the cops you trespassed, then dumped the blue roan and stormed off, driving like a maniac. We tell them it was an accident waiting to happen.'

All too easily Kirstie pictured the scene. She sat slumped on Moondance, feeling her nerve drain away as Turner played these mind games. Sensing her distress, the blue roan shifted uneasily on the rocky slope.

But Hadley still held out against what seemed like the inevitable. 'So put away the guns,' he advised. 'No way can you use them in the new scenario.'

'Only against the mare,' Turner conceded. Warning his wrangler to keep Hadley pinned against the rock, he turned his aim on to Moondance.

Now there were two guns pointing at them from a distance of under ten yards, and Hadley had done all he could.

It was the end of the road. The only thing for Kirstie to do was to slide quietly from the horse's back and leave her to her fate. Yet she just couldn't do it.

Moondance stood square, facing Turner, with his second accomplice alongside. Kirstie saw their fingers wrap around their triggers and they steadied their aims, ready to fire.

The pitiful thing was that the horse didn't

understand what was about to happen. A gun was a thing she knew nothing of – the pull of the trigger, the explosion of the bullet out of the barrel . . .

'We shoot whether you get down off her back or not,' Turner warned. 'It's up to you.'

'I stay,' Kirstie told them. No way could she betray Moondance in the last moments of her life. She would wait with her until the shot rang out.

And then what? A futile fight at the cliff edge for their own lives – Hadley and herself against three strong guys. An alibi all ready for the sheriff when he arrived.

Kirstie felt Moondance quiver. It wasn't the mystery guns that suddenly put her on edge, it was a faint sound in the distance drawing quickly nearer. A car engine. A fast driver. Loud enough to spook the horse, approaching rapidly enough to make the men swing round.

As Moondance reared and Kirstie clung to her mane, Hadley escaped from his guard to make a run at Turner. He threw himself around his waist and dragged him to the ground, wrestling for the gun.

The car roared through the entrance, across the ranch yard, heading for the trail Hadley and Turner had just driven.

Kirstie's heart thumped at her ribcage as Moondance's hooves clattered against the smooth pink rock. She felt the horse slither backwards and hung on tight.

Hadley and Turner were on their feet, Hadley had kicked the gun out of reach under a bush. Now Turner's hand was round the old man's throat, throttling him. The two wranglers were rooted to the spot.

Kirstie saw the old man losing the struggle against the young ranch boss. She saw Turner force Hadley up on to the ridge, caught a glimpse of the two men tottering at the edge. Turner was pushing Hadley off balance. Hadley's arms flailed.

And then he dropped out of sight.

Kirstie screamed.

Moondance lost her footing on the rock, her legs gave way and slipped from under her. Together she and Kirstie slid towards the trees.

10

The only way to stay on as Moondance lost her footing and slid down from the ridge was by clinging tight to her mane. Kirstie's fingers were intertwined with the coarse hair, gripping until her knuckles turned white.

They were skidding backwards. Moondance squealed in terror, neck craning forwards, front legs struggling to find some purchase on the solid rock.

Then a boulder knocked them sideways, winding the horse and almost flinging Kirstie from her back. For a split second Kirstie thought that Moondance would roll on to one side and trap her. She would be crushed to death as they continued their downward slide.

But miraculously the mare righted herself before she rolled and by now they were facing downhill, able to see the obstacles ahead. Kirstie threw herself forward and flung her arms round Moondance's neck to avoid the first of several low branches. Underfoot, rock gave way to loose dirt and sprawling, sweet smelling sage.

The soft earth slowed Moondance's involuntary descent. It allowed her to brace her front legs and dig in, throwing up loose stones into Kirstie's face as they continued to slide.

Kirstie narrowed her eyes to keep out the grit. Still she grew aware of the vehicle racing up the track, not Sheriff Francini's patrol car, but a plain black saloon.

Too late! she thought desperately, as she fought to stay on her horse. The new arrivals might be able to act as witnesses and stop Turner from carrying out his threat to shoot Moondance, but poor Hadley was already lying dead at the bottom of a fifty foot drop.

He'd given up his own life to save his horse. Choked by dust and the tears that rose from a lump in her throat and began to stream down her face,

Kirstie felt Moondance finally slew sideways into a tree and come to a halt.

There were no guns in sight as Turner and his two men regrouped and prepared to face the driver of the black saloon.

They acted concerned but innocent, running quickly to report a tragic accident which they hadn't been able to prevent. Meanwhile, shocked to the core, Kirstie slid from Moondance's back on to her knees, giving way to loud sobs as she wrapped her arms around her middle and rocked to and fro.

'Phone for a doctor!' Turner yelled. 'We got one guy involved in a fall over the cliff and a kid trying some crazy bareback stunt on the ridge!'

But he stopped short when the driver of the black car stepped out.

It was Will Ryman, stony faced, hands on hips, waiting for his passenger to emerge.

Kirstie looked up through her tears. At first she shook her head in disbelief. What was Will doing here? And could that be Lisa getting out of the car and standing beside him? Slowly she got to her feet and urged Moondance along so she could find out more.

'Butt out, Ryman!' Ty Turner's tone had changed to a bellow of anger and surprise. 'Didn't I tell you to keep your nose out of my business?'

His two wranglers moved in threateningly on Will and Lisa, one eye on their boss, awaiting orders.

'I warned you!' Turner insisted, thrusting himself between his men and coming up to within inches of Will's impassive face. 'You take one step out of line and I'll make sure you never work in movies again!'

Stumbling towards them with Moondance, Kirstie needed to tell Will and Lisa what had happened to Hadley. She tried to shape a sentence to break the terrible news, yet she backed away from the act, knowing that putting it into words would suddenly make it all the more true.

And the image of Hadley flinging out his arms to try and stop himself from toppling over the edge was burned into her memory. It would stay with her for the rest of her life.

'Yeah, and like a coward I backed off,' Will told Turner. '. . . Like all the other losers who work with you!'

The two wranglers bristled and looked like they wanted to punch and pummel Will until he begged for mercy. But Turner stopped them. He'd glanced

141

at Lisa and spotted the video tape which she held in her hand.

Will smiled wryly. 'Yeah, I give you three guesses what's on the tape.'

Turner grunted then swore.

'That's right,' Will went on. 'It's the out-takes from the Firefly movie. The footage we couldn't use. Like, for instance, the section where you trailered the black stallion down the draw way out on the plains – when your three guys prepared to set him loose and the stallion objected. He reared up and smashed the nearest guy's leg in two separate places, put him in hospital for a week and a half. Yet wasn't that the part when Ty Turner was supposed to prove he was the hero, moving in solo on a so-called wild mustang?'

Once more Turner swore and threatened. He lunged for the tape, but Lisa stepped quickly back and held it out of reach.

'Oh, and then there's the part when you whip the blue roan with the metal end of a lead-rope,' Will reminded him.

'I'll get you!' Turner yelled, beside himself with rage. His normally handsome face was screwed up and ugly, his teeth visible behind a curling snarl.

'You want me to snatch the tape?' the tall ranch hand asked.

'Hey, there's no point!' Lisa cut in, still fiercely protecting the evidence. 'You should know that if Will was smart enough to walk away from his job at Como-Vision with his own copy of the out-takes, then he sure was intelligent enough to back up the original with another copy.'

'. . . Which I mailed to Sheriff Francini late yesterday,' Will added drily. There was satisfaction in his face as he watched Turner take in the implications of what they'd told him.

'Then Will called me and we decided it was time to act,' Lisa said. 'He mentioned the phone call from you, Kirstie; how you'd warned him that Turner was on to him, plus you and Hadley.'

'But why did you call Lisa, Will?' Kirstie cut in.

'I guess I wanted someone to tell me what was the right thing to do,' he admitted quietly.

Lisa took up the account once more. 'I said no way could he lie low and hope to stay out of trouble. His conscience wouldn't let him. That's when he told me he had a secret copy of the tape. I fixed for him to pick me up in San Luis at dawn today and drive out here to lay it on the line. So here we are.'

'And it's all over for you,' Will told Turner.

Enraged, the ranch boss made one final lunge at the tape. This time it was his own guys who pulled him back.

'He's right – it's over,' the gaunt one said, thrusting his ex-boss down into the dirt in disgust. 'I quit!' Striding away down the hill, he was quickly followed by the other.

Their sudden betrayal brought a twisted smile to Turner's lips. 'Rats leaving a sinking ship!' he muttered.

Then he turned on Kirstie, before he set off after them towards the house. 'All this because of some stupid horse!' he yelled, gesturing towards the rocky ridge. 'You ruin me and get a guy killed for the sake of one crazy blue roan!'

'Killed!' The word cut through her like a knife.

'Who got killed? What's he talking about?' Lisa demanded.

Will and Lisa had arrived on the spot too late to see or hear from Turner what had happened to Hadley. So Kirstie had to say the sentence she'd dreaded.

'Hadley fought with Turner,' she told them, gesturing towards the summit. 'There's a fifty foot drop over a sheer cliff into a creek. Turner pushed him clean over. Hadley's dead, Lisa. He died to save Moondance!'

* * *

Will's first reaction was to run to the top of the slope. Kirstie watched him stop short at the dizzy drop into the valley.

'What do you see?' Lisa gasped, sprinting after him once she'd overcome her shock.

Kirstie followed more slowly with Moondance, dreading the sight she would see on the banks of the creek.

'There's a pick-up amongst the trees!' Will yelled over his shoulder.

'Yeah, that's Hadley's,' Lisa confirmed as she drew level and peered down. 'But he wasn't in the car, was he?' she checked with Kirstie, her voice shaky and full of fear.

Kirstie shook her head. 'Nobody could survive that, could they?'

The cliff fell vertically in a smooth, unbroken drop. There was no vegetation to cling to, no ledge to break Hadley's fall. Only at the very bottom did trees find enough soil to take root, and it was these aspens which were partly concealing the old man's wrecked truck.

Will took a long hard look. 'How deep is that creek?' he wondered.

'Hard to say from this distance.' Catching a faint

145

glimmer of hope, Lisa glanced at Kirstie.

'You mean, if it's deep enough, it could've broken his fall?' Kirstie whispered.

Will nodded. 'It's a long shot, so don't get up any serious hopes. But if that creek is swollen by snowmelt from the mountains, and judging by the lie of the land it most likely is, then there could be a chance.'

'And I don't see – well, there's no . . .' Lisa fumbled for words that didn't sound too awful. 'I can't see Hadley lying there!'

No body. Kirstie nodded. 'How do we get down there to take a look?'

All three felt the mounting tension. Don't hope too hard, yet don't count the old wrangler out. He'd led a tough life, survived many a dangerous situation in his time.

'I figure we make our way left along the ridge until we reach the part where the cliff finishes and that more gradual hill takes over,' Will suggested.

The girls looked to see what he meant and saw a change in the landscape about half a mile downstream.

'We take it at an angle,' he went on. 'Not straight down. That way we minimise the steepness of the slope. Eventually we reach the creek.'

'But it'll take forever!' Lisa sighed, at the same time recognising that it was the only thing to do.

Kirstie's heart was pumping hard as she judged the route. 'Not on Moondance,' she argued. 'We could get down in half the time!'

'Without a saddle?' Lisa asked. 'And with no bit – on this crazy horse?'

Kirstie quickly nodded. There was no time to spend discussing the dangers. If Hadley was still alive, they had to reach him fast. So she vaulted smoothly on to Moondance's back and gazed down at Lisa and Will.

'This horse can handle it,' she assured them. 'And I figure she knows the situation. If I take her down into that valley to look for Hadley, she'll give me everything she's got!'

Kirstie was right about the blue roan's willingness to tackle the difficult terrain, in spite of her recent, terrifying slide down the slickrock.

Moondance and Kirstie set off ahead of Will and Lisa who soon lagged way behind. The mare listened intently to what her bareback rider wanted her to do, trotting parallel to the jagged ridge along the safer surface of grit and sage bush. Her ears twitched and turned, responding to orders from

Kirstie and looking out for hazards ahead. Skirting thorn bushes, picking her way between rocks, they soon reached the point on the horizon where Kirstie judged they should turn up the hill and crest the ridge.

'C'mon, girl, let's do it!' she breathed, sensing Moondance's reluctance. 'Yeah, I know it's scary. But when we get to the top this time, we don't meet a sheer drop. We find a slope we can manage and we pick our way down.' Coaxing in a gentle voice, trying to still the rapid beating of her own heart, Kirstie persuaded the mare to recross the band of rock on to the ridge.

And there below was the slope she'd hoped for, steep but possible for Moondance to take at a slow walk. The horse agreed, going more willingly now, letting her own weight slide her gently down the gritty surface, swaying her rear end for better balance. Kirstie hung on tight to her mane, letting her choose her own route, trusting her.

But the whole thing was still getting to Kirstie – the danger to her and her horse, the prospect of what they might find when they finally reached the creek. She had to grit her teeth to keep this image from flooding her mind. *Think positive!* she told herself. Ignore the roar of the water as it swept between high rocks in a narrow, foaming channel. Believe that luck had been with Hadley when he fell.

Now rising spray reached them and settled in a fine, cold mist on Kirstie's cheeks. The volume of the water rushing through the creek grew until it drowned out the questioning voices of Lisa and Will from above.

Kirstie glanced back through a thin canopy of silver green leaves and shook her head. She guessed they'd been asking if she could see any sign of Hadley. *No, nothing!*

Only white water foaming over rocks, deep currents sucking driftwood from the whirling surface and dragging it down out of sight.

Kirstie shook her head again. No way would anyone survive this stretch of water. But if she and Moondance could find a way upstream and around a bend to reach the spot where Hadley had fallen, then maybe, just maybe they would hit a wider, calmer section of the creek.

It meant picking their way along the very edge of the bank, where the rocks were slimy with moss. But Moondance forged on, growing more surefooted as she went, seeming to have figured out for herself the reason why they were doing this.

'That's right, we've gotta find Hadley!' Kirstie urged, her hair wet with spray, her soaked T-shirt and jeans clinging to her skin.

And it seemed as if the current was stronger and wilder than ever as they went into the bend. The water smashed against the far bank and came crashing towards them, cascading heavy white spray over them as they trod a narrow ledge of rock.

Then they were round the sharp spur of land, facing a new wide stretch of gently flowing water where the sunlight filtered through the trees and the current swirled lazily towards them.

Yes! Kirstie's heart gladdened at the sight. She glanced up at the sheer cliff, and by the shape of the horizon picked out the point where Turner had fought and pushed Hadley over the edge.

'Only a little bit further!' she promised Moondance.

But the horse already knew that. She picked up her pace along a grassy, even stretch of bank, ears pricked forward, eyes fixed on a point twenty yards ahead.

'Easy, girl!' Kirstie murmured as her horse stumbled down a hidden hollow.

Moondance regained her balance and pressed on.

There was a tree ahead, its trunk slanting over the creek at a point where the water was so deep that it looked almost black. The aspen branches hung low, trailing their leaves in the creek. And there was a fork in the main trunk which faced upstream and was within reach of anyone swimming in the gentle current.

There was something – someone – wedged in that fork. The hatless, grey-haired figure had hooked his arms over the trunk and let his legs trail with the current. The head and shoulders were slumped forward, so that at first Kirstie thought that the body was lifeless.

She groaned out loud. Moondance's hooves hit hard rock and rang out.

Then Hadley lifted his head. 'You and that blue roan took your time,' he complained. 'My ankle's busted and this left shoulder ain't good for nothin'. For Pete's sake, get me outta here!'

'You know what he's like!' Kirstie told Brad in Denver hospital on the day that the good news about his own injury came through. The damage to his neck and spine had been declared temporary – the contusions and swellings were healing, returning movement to his legs and arms. The

medics had assured him and Sandy that Brad and Little Vixen would soon be back in the competition ring.

Now Kirstie told them about Hadley's involuntary swim in Aspen Creek.

'I save the guy's life by dragging him out of the water, and all he can do is complain!'

Brad smiled from his wheelchair. 'Typical Hadley,' he agreed.

'He's got a broken leg and a smashed shoulder from where he fell fifty feet and hit the water. But all the time Moondance and I are wading waist high to lift him off the tree branch and get him back on dry land he's asking who's gonna repay him for the cost of his wrecked truck!' Kirstie remembered all this with a wry grin.

Will and Lisa had joined her on the bank and they'd phoned for an air ambulance to lift Hadley out. They'd seen him safely whisked off to Denver then climbed out of the valley back to the ranch in time to see Sheriff Francini drive off with Ty Turner in handcuffs.

'He oughta get Turner to pay out for a new Dodge,' Brad suggested.

'Some hope!' Sandy shrugged. 'From what the sheriff told me, Turner's in no shape to put his hands on any cash for some time to come. They froze the income on the Firefly movie and his wranglers closed up the dude ranch. Turner himself is in gaol, facing a charge of attempted homicide.'

So that was OK. Kirstie gave a satisfied nod, then stood up. 'I guess I'd best go visit the old guy and see how he's doing.'

'Tell him from me, he's to follow doctors' orders!' Sandy called after her.

Some hope! Kirstie repeated to herself. Down the corridor in another trauma room, Hadley was undergoing treatment for his ankle and shoulder.

'How're you goin' with the trainin' sessions?' he demanded the moment she walked in.

Kirstie took a seat. 'Moondance is doing fine,' she assured him. 'She acts like an angel, even when I show her the lead-rope. I can get her saddle on her no problem and ride her round the arena doing lead changes and even a couple of sliding stops.'

'Hmm.' Strapped up and immobilised on his bed, Hadley's response gave nothing away. Robbed of his stetson and working clothes, which had been replaced by dressings and hospital gown, he looked frail and old.

'But I guess Moondance is missing you,' Kirstie added quickly.

Hadley sniffed.

'She doesn't settle so easy in her stall at night without a visit from you,' she insisted. 'And she spends all day looking around to see where you got to.'

'She eatin' OK?' he checked.

'Yep.'

Silence. Hadley let her know that the short visit was over. He'd found out everything he needed to know. Now he wanted to sleep.

Kirstie stood up and got ready to leave.

'Hey!' the old man said after she'd taken two or three steps towards the door.

She turned.

'I guess I ought to thank you,' he mumbled.

'No problem,' Kirstie replied, suddenly embarrassed. She set off again until his drawling voice stopped her a second time.

He looked her full in the face, gratitude still lingering in his eyes. 'And you take good care of that blue roan, you hear?'

'Sure will!' she agreed, glancing at her wristwatch. It was time to hightail it back to Half-Moon Ranch and work some more with Moondance.

HORSES OF HALF-MOON RANCH 15
Lady Roseanne

Jenny Oldfield

Matt's new girlfriend, Lauren, has gone on a study trip and left her beautiful horse, Lady Roseanne, at Half-Moon Ranch. Keen to impress, Matt pays lots of attention to the appaloosa mare. So he loses it big-time when he finds lovely Lady covered in cuts and scratches. He blames the new wrangler, Karina Cooper – but Kirstie suspects someone or something else is to blame . . .